Mallory found herself staring into a pair of deep blue eyes.

A strikingly familiar blue.

She froze. Her lips parted, but no words could emerge, since her mouth had gone bone-dry.

He was the one to break the silence, his voice deep and slightly gruff and definitely in keeping with his rough, unshaven jaw and the tousled dark hair on his head that looked in need of a good barber. "*You're* Dr. Keegan?"

She swallowed. Nodded.

His gaze was sharp. Studying. Almost as if he were memorizing her appearance before he stuck out a bare, long-fingered hand. "I'm Ryan Clay."

Her hand seemed to rise of its own accord and settle against his for the briefest of moments.

The contact still managed to leave her feeling shaky.

And that shakiness had nothing to do with the words that she knew were going to come out of his mouth, before they actually did.

"I'm here about your daughter."

Dear Reader,

Every month I receive letters or e-mails from readers asking about various members of the Clay family, or wanting an update on what's going on at the Double-C Ranch or in Weaver. I have a really large collection from those who've wanted to know *what's* been going on with Ryan. Where is he? Is he coming back? Is he dead? Is he alive?

As an author it is so rewarding to know that these people have found a place where they're welcomed and cared about—like members of a family. That's how they are in *my* mind, and it's wonderful to know I'm not alone!

Well, I'm happy to say Ryan is, indeed, quite alive, and never more so than when he encounters the Keegan women, and he discovers that there is existing…and then there is living.

He's been through a lot, our Ryan. But now he's back for good. I hope you enjoy the homecoming.

All my best,

Allison

A WEAVER
HOLIDAY
HOMECOMING

ALLISON LEIGH

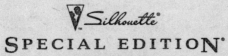

SPECIAL EDITION

Published by Silhouette Books

America's Publisher of Contemporary Romance

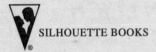

SILHOUETTE BOOKS

ISBN-13: 978-0-373-65497-0

Recycling programs
for this product may
not exist in your area.

A WEAVER HOLIDAY HOMECOMING

Printed in U.S.A.

ALLISON LEIGH

started early by writing a Halloween play that her grade-school class performed. Since then, though her tastes have changed, her love for reading has not. And her writing appetite simply grows more voracious by the day.

She has been a finalist for the RITA® Award and the Holt Medallion. But the true highlights of her day as a writer are when she receives word from a reader that they laughed, cried or lost a night of sleep while reading one of her books.

Born in Southern California, Allison has lived in several different cities in four different states. She has been, at one time or another, a cosmetologist, a computer programmer and a secretary. She has recently begun writing full-time after spending nearly a decade as an administrative assistant for a busy neighborhood church. She currently makes her home in Arizona with her family. She loves to hear from her readers, who can write to her at P.O. Box 40772, Mesa, AZ 85274-0772.

This is for all of you who've kept asking for Ryan's story. Thank you for your patience!

Prologue

"This isn't an assignment like anything else you've ever done. That we've ever done." The silver-haired man watched him steadily from across the small table. "There are even fewer guarantees than usual."

Around them, the small backwater pub was crowded with people. No one seemed interested in what any of the other patrons were doing. Or discussing. This wasn't the kind of place where people came to be seen.

It was the kind of place where people came to remain invisible.

Which was why it was a perfect meeting place for Ryan Clay and his boss.

He eyed the older man who'd just outlined the dicey undercover scheme and slowly twisted his glass in the ring of sweat the ice had left on the scarred wooden tabletop. "I can handle it," he said, since Cole seemed to be waiting for some sort of response.

"It's not going to be easy," Cole warned.

Needlessly.

Nothing to do with the agency had ever been easy. It hadn't been for any of the agents on Hollins-Winword's very secretive payroll—several of whom came from Ryan's own family.

And it was family that had grabbed his interest when Coleman Black gave Ryan the rundown. How many families were being destroyed by the trafficking ring he was being assigned to infiltrate?

"I can handle it," he said again. A little impatiently, because if his boss hadn't already known that point, he wouldn't have chosen to offer Ryan the assignment in the first place. Coleman Black was a hard-as-nails man. But he was also practical. He didn't like losing good agents. They were too hard to come by.

By the time an agent got to the level Ryan held within the organization, assignments weren't doled out by demand. They were offered. And always with the expectation that it was no sin for the agent to decline.

Mostly, because some agents never made it back.

Ryan easily pushed the thought out of his mind and met his boss's sharp gaze. "Let's just get on with it."

Coleman watched him for a moment longer. Measuring.

Then he nodded. He sat forward. And then their low talk began in earnest.

Chapter One

Five years later.

*H*e couldn't handle it.

Ryan Clay stared into the black depths of his coffee mug, wishing it were whiskey—except he'd given that up a year ago—and thought about all the ways he could escape.

The simplest way, of course, would be to just disappear. Again.

It had worked before. For a while. The fact that he still felt guilty for letting everyone who loved him think the worst was beside the point. Better for them to have thought he'd perished doing the honorable thing—living up to the Clay family standards—than knowing the truth.

That he'd walked away from a mission without finishing it, and he'd done it with blood on his hands.

But if he really believed that, then why the hell had he

come back at all? He could have stayed right where he was…in a corner of the world surrounded by people equally miserable as he.

He hooked his boot heel over the rung on his counter stool and lifted the coffee mug. Grimaced as he swallowed.

"You sure you don't want a refill?" Tabby Taggart stopped on the other side of the counter, holding the coffee carafe aloft. "You've been nursing that cup for an hour now, Ryan. Gotta be cold."

It was.

Cold and bitter.

Pretty much just like he was.

"No. Thanks," he tacked on. The last time he'd seen Tabby, she'd been a high school kid. It didn't seem as if she'd changed much. She was still a kid to him, seeming aeons younger than his thirty-seven, but he knew she was already out of college. Waiting tables at Ruby's while she tried for some fancy position at an Italian museum.

Nor had Ruby's Diner changed much in all the years he'd been coming there. Not since his mother had moved them to the small town of Weaver, Wyoming, when he'd been nine.

The chrome-padded stools at the counter were still topped with shining red vinyl. The booths lining the square room were still full of people. The most popular item, though, wasn't even on the menu.

Gossip.

He could just imagine what the wagging tongues would end up making over his presence *here* in the diner. Alone. Again.

Like he'd been at Colbys bar the night before. And the night before that.

They could add it to the oddity of him staying at the Sleep Tite motel since he'd come back to town, instead of staying with his folks or any one of his plentiful relatives.

He pressed a fingertip to the pain throbbing behind his right eyebrow. Closing his eyes for a minute, he tried to block out the clatter of flatware against sturdy white crockery, the tinny Christmas carols and the conversations—mostly seeming to focus on what so-and-so was doing or the town's upcoming Holiday Festival. There'd been a time when he could turn off every distraction and focus only on a single thought, a single quest, a single goal.

"Hey there, Chloe." He heard Tabby's cheerful voice and opened his eyes again to stare into his black coffee. He was vaguely aware of the dark-haired little girl who'd come up to the counter to stand a few feet away from him. She'd been sitting in the corner booth with a small-framed old woman with white sausage-curls covering her head.

"Grammy and I want to take Mom a piece of pie," the kid was saying. "That one." She pointed a slender finger at the glass-enclosed pie case that was draped with silver-and-red garland, but Ryan could feel the sideways glance the kid gave him as Tabby assured the child that she'd wrap up the slice, and began pulling the pie out of the case.

"She don't like pumpkin," the kid told Ryan as if he had indicated some interest. "It's a surprise."

He managed to twist his lips into a smile that he hoped wouldn't scare her.

She was cute—dressed in purple from head to toe with the exception of her lime-green snow boots—and he'd had enough in his lifetime of scared little girls.

"If she likes pecan pie, she'd probably like the cinnamon rolls here, too." From the corner of his eye he caught the glance Tabby gave him. She looked only slightly less surprised at his comment than he felt. "They're loaded with pecans."

"Dr. Keegan's already discovered them," Tabby offered, sliding a small pink box across the counter toward the little girl, along with an easy smile. "I think she might like them almost as much as you."

The little girl—Chloe—turned her bright eyes toward Ryan again. The edge of her small, white teeth nibbled at her pink lower lip as she looked at the lone mug sitting in front of him. "Arntcha hungry? There's still some left." She pointed at the remaining pie that Tabby was putting back into the case.

It's what he got for giving an opening. Pint-size conversation. "No." He tried softening the terse word with a smile of sorts and probably failed miserably, judging by the way the kid started chewing her lip again.

"So the pie is a surprise for your mom?" Tabby filled the silence before it could turn awkward and the girl nodded as she pulled a wad of crumpled cash and a few coins out of the front pocket of her purple jeans.

"Uh-huh." This time when the tip of Chloe's tongue appeared between her lips, it was in concentration as she smoothed the dollar bills and carefully counted out the change. "She hadda work even on a Saturday. So Grammy and I were Christmas shopping."

Tabby leaned her arms on the counter, smiling conspiratorially. "Where'd you go?"

"All over." The kid bounced up and down on the heels of her snow boots. "But the bestest place was the thrift store in Braden. I got Mom's present there and *still* had allowance left." She slanted Ryan a look. "I gotta earn it dusting," she confided. "I saved every week." Chloe's thin shoulders went up and down in a huge sigh. "It wasn't 'nuff, though. Not to get the video game I wanted, too. It's the *new* Purple Princess. Right there at the thrift store. It was only twenty dollars." Her wide eyes still held amazement. "It's over *fifty* at the regular store."

"Christmas is in three weeks," Ryan couldn't help pointing out. "Put it on your letter to Santa." He figured she was still young enough to believe in that particular Christmas miracle.

"My birthday's before Christmas." She held up seven fingers, managing not to drop the cash wadded in her palm in the process. "I'll be seven. But Mom says it's still too 'spensive. I'm going to have a birthday party, though. With seven of my new friends. I never had a birthday party before."

"Chloe, dear." The white-haired woman from the corner booth was waiting near the door. "You've visited long enough and your mama's probably waiting by now. Come on now."

"Comin' Grammy." Chloe fumbled with the cash, pushing it into her pocket before scooping up the pie box. "Thanks, Tabby." She shot Ryan a look. "Nice t'meet you, mister." She turned on her toes with a squeak of her rubbery boots. "Looks like you dropped something," she added in a rush before she joined her grandmother at the door and scooted out into the afternoon.

Ryan frowned a little, watching the elderly woman and the child for a moment before turning back to his cold coffee. But the clatter of crockery and impossibly cheerful Christmas music suddenly felt like a fine edge cutting into his brain and he dropped a bill on the counter beside it and slid off the stool. "See you later, Tab."

Already busy pouring coffee for another customer, she lifted her free hand in a wave.

He didn't notice the dollar bill by his boot on the floor until he hooked his jacket off the empty stool beside his and turned toward the door.

He stared at it for a moment. He knew he hadn't dropped it. The smallest bills in his pocket were twenties.

The brown-haired, blue-eyed girl had dropped it. Claimed it to be his.

He ran his hand down his jaw, absently aware of the rasp of whiskers. Shaving hadn't been high on his list lately.

He looked bad enough that an innocent kid figured he needed a handout and was cagey enough to mask the charity out of her hard-earned dusting money.

He swallowed an oath and leaned over to swipe up the

dollar in his fist, then turned back to the counter. "Tabby. The little girl. Chloe. What do you know about her?"

Tabby shrugged and wiped her hands on a damp towel. "Her mom is Mallory Keegan. The O.B. who's filling in over at Doc Yarnell's practice while he's on sabbatical. The office is over on Sycamore," she added when he gave her a blank look.

The street he knew. The name of the doctor, he didn't. Ryan could remember a time when his mother was the only doctor in the area. Now she ran the Weaver hospital, and the town had enough obstetrical needs to support a doctor who could go on sabbatical.

Some things did change.

"Thanks." He shrugged into his jacket and left.

Outside, the afternoon was cold, the sky overhead heavy with gray clouds. Looking one way, he could see the sheriff's office. For more years than Ryan could remember, his father had been the sheriff. He'd retired several years ago—back when Ryan had been MIA—but he couldn't look at the brick building now, without thinking about his dad.

Both of Ryan's parents had been plainly happy when he'd returned from the dead. As had the rest of the family. To them, it had been a miracle.

Ryan, though, still felt dead.

No miracle.

No honor.

He pulled out a cigarette, lighting it as he turned the opposite direction from that stalwart brick building of law and order and flipped up his collar. Sycamore was just two streets down from Main, but it was a long street—and God only knew where the doctor's office was. It could be close—here in the original, older part of Weaver. Or it could be out in the newer part of town where a crop of apartment buildings had sprung up during the years of his absence, along with a giant Shop-World and a gaggle of other stores.

Some things hadn't changed in Weaver. And some things had. But Ryan was willing to bet that he'd be able to find Chloe Keegan by the time the afternoon was out.

He'd spent three years trying—and too often failing—to save girls not all that much older than Chloe from being sold off to the highest bidder. The last thing his conscience needed right now was the additional weight of some little kid with a soft heart.

"Mom!"

Mallory Keegan lifted her head at the hollered greeting, only to smack it smartly against the inside frame of the cabinet she was presently tucked halfway inside. She muttered an oath even as the wrench slid out of her hand, clanging loudly against the water pipe.

The pipe that she had *just* managed to get to stop leaking.

So much for that.

She swiped her hand over the fine mist of water that spurted anew from the pipes, spraying her right in the face and backed out of the cupboard.

"Upstairs," she yelled back down to her daughter as she grabbed the bath towel off the rack on the wall behind her. She dashed it down her face and then tossed it over the thin but copious spray.

She collected Pap smears and delivered babies.

She did *not* fix plumbing of this sort at all.

Which meant she'd have to add a plumber's repair bill to the budget that month. A budget that was already tight, particularly with Chloe's birthday and Christmas looming.

She could hear her daughter's boots clomping rapidly up the stairs but the long day—an unexpected cesarean for a third-time mom and a miscarriage for a first-timer—had her tiredly sitting back on her heels and just waiting.

It didn't take long.

Chloe careened around the corner of the bathroom, a small pink bakery box clutched against the midriff of her purple sweatshirt. Her boots slid a little, squeaking against the hardwood floor that still bore the dampness that Mallory hadn't succeeded in wiping away.

The sight of her daughter's face, wreathed in smiles, was enough to counter her exhaustion, though, and she opened her arms just in time to stop Chloe's momentum in a hug. The feel of her daughter's strong, sturdy little body was enough to melt her frustration.

The bakery box knocked against Mallory's head as Chloe's arms wound around her neck. "Didja have any babies today?"

Long used to Chloe's bursts of speech, Mallory laughed a little. "I *delivered* a baby today," she said, and caught the box that was in danger of being crushed altogether. "What's this?"

Chloe straightened. "Pie." She stuck her head under the sink. "Is it fixed?"

"Don't move the—" Mallory could tell the moment Chloe's curiosity prompted her to move the towel from the pipe, because she squeaked and jumped back out of the indoor sprinkler "—towel," she finished.

Her daughter wasn't a large fan of water in her face. She tolerated her baths out of necessity, but anything more— swimming, splashing in a sprinkler on a hot, summer day— was mostly out of the question.

But Mallory hadn't temporarily uprooted her family from New York to settle in this small Wyoming town for the purpose of getting Chloe over her fear of water.

Her reasoning had been much more involved.

"Here." She pushed aside the disquiet that was all too willing to coil anxiously in her stomach these days, and handed Chloe another towel off the towel rack.

She dropped the wet towel back over the leaking pipe and

pushed to her feet. "It's going to take a person who actually knows what they're doing to fix it, I'm afraid."

She steered Chloe out of the bathroom toward the stairs and peeked into the bakery box at the enormous pecan-laden wedge of pie. Her mouth watered. Between the hospital and the leaking pipe, she hadn't managed to find time for a decent meal. "Looks delicious." She leaned down and kissed the top of Chloe's nut-brown hair, spotting her grandmother when they reached the foot of the stairs and turned to the kitchen. "Thank you," she told them both.

"Thank her." After less than two decades in the United States, Kathleen Keegan's voice still held plenty of her native Ireland as she waved at Chloe. "She paid for it out of her allowance."

Mallory set the pie on the narrow breakfast bar and found a fork in the drawer. "Did you have fun shopping before you stopped for lunch?" Kathleen was notorious for finding bargains in the oddest of places.

She looked up as she sank the fork into the rich dessert and caught the secretive glance Chloe and Kathleen shared. "All right, you two. What'd you buy?"

"Nothing." Chloe's voice was innocent, but her eyebrows were riding an inch above normal, hiding beneath the tousled bangs covering her forehead. "I found a Purple Princess game, though. The new one. It was only twenty dollars!"

Mallory hid a smile and tried not to groan in pleasure as she swallowed the forkful of gooey pecan. Chloe adored Purple Princess video games and could endlessly wax eloquent about the reasons why she just "had-had-*had*" to have each new one when they came out. And usually, the games came at a much higher price tag. "Why didn't you buy it, then? I know you had more than twenty dollars in your wallet when you and Grammy started out this morning." And Mallory could have returned the unopened game that she'd already purchased and hidden high in the closet.

Chloe's gaze darted to her grandmother again. Her round cheeks turned rosy. "I gotta go to the bathroom," she suddenly announced, and darted out of the kitchen.

Mallory eyed Kathleen. "Well?"

"Aye, don't be looking at me, child." Kathleen waved her hand in a shooing motion. "I'm not going to blab on her secrets."

Mallory's smile broke loose. "Christmas shopping, perhaps?"

"I'm going to have to hire a plumber," Mallory said, returning to the most pressing issue when Kathleen merely smiled.

"Call your nice Dr. Clay and ask her to recommend someone."

Mallory gnawed the inside of her lip. Prevailing on Rebecca Clay was something she wanted to avoid and not merely because Mallory could guess who the woman would recommend for the job. It was because of the other woman that they were in Weaver at all.

She could hear Chloe's footsteps from overhead.

Well, it wasn't precisely Rebecca Clay that was the reason Mallory and her crew had come to Weaver six weeks ago. Rebecca had just facilitated it.

The real reason was Chloe.

The anxiety inside Mallory swamped her hunger, and she covered the remainder of the pie and rinsed her fork at the sink. "I'll find someone," she murmured as she headed to her office at the back of the house. But the squawking sound of the ancient doorbell had her changing course.

She pushed up the sleeves of her sweater, which were damp from the water leak, and yanked open the heavy door without any of the caution she would have normally used in her apartment building back in New York.

The tall, broad-shouldered man standing there on the porch staring at the ground raised his head as the door swung open, and she found herself looking into a pair of deeply blue eyes.

A strikingly familiar blue.

She froze. Her lips parted, but no words could emerge,

since her mouth had gone bone-dry. No amount of mental preparations had been enough, she realized. Meeting the man in person had been her plan. Her goal. Yet faced with him now, she felt unprepared. Not at *all* ready.

His heavy, dark eyebrows quirked together for a moment, but he was still the one to break the silence, his voice deep and slightly gruff and definitely in keeping with his rough, unshaven jaw and the tousled, dark hair on his head that looked in need of a good barber. "*You're* Dr. Keegan?"

She swallowed. Nodded.

His gaze was sharp. Studying. Almost as if he were memorizing her appearance before he stuck out a bare, long-fingered hand. "I'm Ryan Clay," he introduced with spare brevity.

Her hand seemed to lift of its own accord and settle against his square palm for the briefest of moments.

The contact still managed to leave her feeling shaky.

And that shakiness had nothing to do with the words that she knew were going to come out of his mouth, before they actually did.

"I'm here about your daughter."

Chapter Two

It was almost like looking at a ghost, Ryan thought, staring at the woman. Dr. Keegan.

She was staring back at him, her eyes wide. They were distinct, those eyes. A honey-brown that was oddly translucent.

And oddly familiar, though he knew for a fact that he'd never met her before.

"What about my daughter?" Her smooth voice had a faint lilt to it. And though it might have held suspicion, given the way he was showing up on her doorstep like this, it didn't seem to.

But it held something. Something he couldn't quite identify.

He realized she was hugging her arms across her chest; the white cable-knit sweater she wore not doing enough to hold the cold air at bay. "I want to return this." He held out the dollar bill that Chloe had left. "And give her this." He pulled an envelope out of his coat pocket.

The doctor moistened her lips, drawing attention that didn't need to be drawn considering he'd already taken note of their shape. Their soft fullness. The fact that they were bare, pale pink.

The envelope crinkled softly between his fingers.

God. She was so damn familiar—

"Mom! Grammy said to tell you the water in the bathroom's getting worse." Chloe suddenly appeared next to her mother, sliding between the doctor's slender body and the door. Her smile widened when she spotted him. "Hi. What are you doing here?"

Her mom's hand slid over the girl's shoulder, closing protectively across her chest.

He didn't blame the woman. Kids needed protection in this world. Even in little towns like Weaver, Wyoming.

He crouched down until he was more on a level with the kid and handed her the dollar bill. "This is yours. I really didn't need it as much as you thought."

She didn't take it, though her spiky black lashes lowered and her eyes shied away guiltily. "No, it's not."

"Chloe? What's going on?"

Ryan looked up at the doctor. It had been easy enough to track them down to this old house in this old neighborhood. Once he'd found the office on Sycamore, all he'd had to do was visit a few of the neighboring businesses to ask about the new doctor in town, and tongues had started wagging.

Before long, he'd learned all about the house she'd rented about six weeks ago near the town park; the fact that she was friendly but not too; that her daughter was attending school and the grandmother helped watch the girl.

None of the talkative souls he'd run into had mentioned a man in the mix.

"Your daughter has a generous heart, Dr. Keegan."

She tucked a wave of streaky brown hair behind her ear. "Mallory," she said faintly. "And, yes. She does. But I'm afraid I don't understand what this is about."

"Here." Since the kid wouldn't take the dollar, he stuffed it into the mom's hand instead and handed the kid the envelope, which she tore into eagerly as he rose to face the mom again. Though that was a relative term, since Mallory Keegan stood damn near a foot shorter than he did. "Your daughter and I ran into each other at Ruby's. She thought I needed a…loan," he settled on.

"Look, Mom!" Chloe had pulled out the gift certificate from the envelope and was waving it between them. "It's for the new Purple Princess game! That's what it says, right? F—r—e—e," she spelled out.

Mallory's brows drew together and she tugged the vivid, purple card he'd picked up at CeeVid—his uncle's computer gaming company—out of her daughter's grasp, looking from Ryan's face to it. "Yes, that's what it says." She focused on Ryan again. Uncertainty clouded her gaze as if she were waging some internal debate.

He wasn't sure who was on the winning side, though, when she took a step back, leaning against the open door to push it wider. Her arm was still around Chloe, the dollar crumpled between her fingers. "Maybe you'd better come in."

He could see past them both into the warmth of the house.

He'd returned the buck. Given the kid a gift just because it was easily convenient for him, thanks to family connections, and it was time to go.

He shifted sideways a little and stepped past her, into the house.

He immediately spotted the white-haired woman from the diner, coming down the stairs. Her arms were full of bath towels. Sopping wet, judging by the water dripping off them.

Mallory pushed back her hair again and gave him an awkward smile. "Have a seat." She waved in the general direction of a living room opening off the hallway where they stood. "Chloe, sit with Mr. Clay and introduce your grand-mother. I'll be back in a moment."

She hurried over to the elderly woman and took the towels. Water squished out of them even more during the exchange, and she left a wet trail behind her as she disappeared down the hall.

Realizing he was watching the sway of her shapely jean-clad rear, he nearly jumped out of his skin when a small, slightly damp hand slid into his.

"Come on." Chloe tugged him toward one of the sleek beige couches that nearly consumed the living room, their style screaming modern against the aged brick of the fireplace that they flanked. "Grammy, this is Mr. Clay," the little girl called over her shoulder as they went. "Mr. Clay, this is Grammy."

He caught the amused glint in the woman's eyes as she followed them. "Kathleen Keegan," the lady elaborated in a distinct brogue. "Can I take your coat?"

The hairs at the nape of his neck prickled. He suddenly felt surrounded by women.

Ordinarily, that wasn't exactly a situation to cause him undue strain. But something about the Keegan women—all three of them—made him distinctly edgy.

He should have just let the kid give up her dollar. She'd have felt good about donating to a charity case and he wouldn't be standing there wondering what the hell he was doing.

But as soon as the wish crossed his thoughts, what was left of his conscience smacked him hard.

So instead of keeping the coat exactly where it was—*on* and ready for him to make a quick exit—he shrugged out of the scarred leather and handed it over to the old woman, who beamed at him as if he were four and had just correctly recited the alphabet.

"Sit. Sit." She waited until he'd perched on the awful couch. "What can I get you to warm yourself?"

He caught sight of Mallory crossing the hallway again and

squelched the wholly inappropriate answer he could have given. "Nothing, ma'am. I'm fine, thank you."

He could see the argument forming in her eyes even before he finished speaking, and pushed to his feet. "Sorry. I don't mean to be nosy, but do you need help?"

He scooted around Kathleen to intercept Mallory. She was carrying a bucket and a mop, with another towel, dry this time, tossed over her shoulder. "Do you have a water leak or something?" Chloe had said something about water getting worse—he hadn't paid any attention because he'd been too busy cataloguing her mother's soft lips, *and* his unwelcome and very physical reaction to her appeal.

Mallory shook her head. "No worries. Everything's fine."

It wasn't exactly an answer and he gave a pointed look at the items in her hands and her cheeks went pinker than her lips.

"Just some cleanup," she added hurriedly, and fairly dashed around him to pound up the stairs. "Gram, fix him some of your famous hot chocolate," she called over her shoulder.

"It's a fine mix," Kathleen said, behind him. "I add a little kick when it's a strapping young man like yourself drinking it."

He didn't want hot chocolate. Even if it were spiked. He didn't want to be here in this house that smelled like lemon furniture polish and lilacs. He didn't want to be reminded of things that were good and clean and worthy.

He wanted to be away from Weaver, away from everything that he'd once known and cared about.

He closed his hand over the newel post at the base of the staircase and looked back at Kathleen. "How bad's the leak?"

She was still holding his coat, folded at her waist. "Pretty bad," she said. Her eyes—a color she'd passed on to Mallory—twinkled a little. "My granddaughter won't admit it, but I'm afraid she might be making it worse."

"Hold the kick," he told Kathleen.

"Can I have some hot chocolate, too, Grammy?" Chloe piped as he headed up the stairs.

Finding the bathroom wasn't difficult. All he had to do was follow the trail of wet footprints down the hardwood hall.

She was on her hands and knees, derriere to the door, furiously wielding the fresh towel over the floor. The source of the problem was obvious thanks to the opened cabinet that had been emptied of everything except a pitiful collection of wrenches and a bucket that was near to full beneath the steady trickle of water coming from one of the pipes.

"Galvanized pipe," he said, and her head jerked around to peer at him over her shoulder.

He leaned his shoulder against the doorjamb and forced himself to look at the plumbing and not the very feminine shape before him.

He mostly failed, though.

"Old houses like this often still have galvanized instead of copper or PVC," he continued. "Unfortunately, it corrodes from the inside out and you sometimes don't even know you've got a problem until—" he waved his hand toward the cabinet and sink "—Niagara Falls."

Her lips compressed and she turned back to drying the floor. "I've tightened again and again. It just won't stop."

He crouched down next to her, realizing too late just how close that would put them. "You need a repair clamp."

She twisted around until she was sitting on her rear. Her shoulder brushed his. "A repair clamp?"

She had a tiny mole above her lip.

He shifted slightly. Put a few inches between them.

He didn't need hot chocolate.

He needed a cold shower.

"Tightens around the pipe with a rubber gasket," he said abruptly.

She looked back at the pipe. Her waving hair slid over her shoulder. Brushed her cheek. "And it stops the leak?"

"Yeah." He shoved to his feet, edging back out of the doorway. Into the hall. Where breathing in didn't mean breathing in the scent of her. "Hardware store'll have them. Doesn't solve the corrosion, though. You'll want a plumber to look into that soon or you might end up with a few more waterfalls before you're through."

She tossed the towel over the leak, pulled the large bucket out to empty into the bathtub, replaced it beneath the leak again and spread the towel out on top of the sink to dry. "I should have rented an apartment in that complex on the other side of town," she muttered, turning to face him. She dusted her hands down her thighs. "I'm used to apartments. I *like* apartments. They come with building superintendents to deal with all of this sort of stuff."

"Then why choose this old place?" She'd have been across town, instead of practically around the block from the Sleep Tite, if she'd have gone the apartment route. "I grew up in this town. The houses in this neighborhood were old when *I* was a kid."

She tilted her head back a little, looking up at the ceiling. "Because I'm a sucker for my family. And both Chloe and Gram loved it on sight. Gram because of the enamel doorknobs and crystal chandelier and Chloe because of the park down the street." She sighed a little and looked back at him. "It seemed the least I could do since it was my decision to uproot them from New York." Her eyes narrowed a little. "I'm sorry. You're not interested in all that. Why did Chloe give you a dollar?"

Like it or not—and he pretty much was squarely in the *not* camp—he was interested in "all that."

Maybe because there was that nagging familiarity about her. Or maybe it was just because every time he looked at her, his blood stirred in a way that it hadn't in a very long time.

Or maybe it was because his own existence was so freaking pathetic that he was dreaming up excuses to prove otherwise.

He shoved his hands into his pockets. Above her head, he could see his reflection in the ancient mirror above the sink. Lines around his eyes. More gray in his unkempt hair than had been there a year ago. A jaw that hadn't seen a razor in too many days.

"She didn't so much as give it to me as pretend it was mine," he said. "She seemed to think I was more in need of her dusting money than she was." He couldn't think of an earthly reason why he was telling her the details. Knowing he'd looked derelict enough to elicit pity from her daughter wasn't exactly something for him to feel proud of.

She was looking at him again. Her amber-colored eyes measured. "Mr. Clay—Ryan—there's something about Chloe you need to know."

He knew enough. She had a tender little heart that he hoped she never had reason to toughen. But, of course, she was only six years old. Life would add calluses sooner or later. "A dollar's not much, I know—"

"It is to her." Mallory moistened her lips again. "And it was very kind of you to return it. I already put it back in her piggy bank. The gift certificate wasn't necessary, though."

He shrugged it off. "She talked about the game at the diner. My uncle owns CeeVid."

She looked blank.

"The company that produces the video game."

"That's here?" Her eyebrows shot up. "In *Weaver?*"

"You really haven't been here long at all, have you?" She couldn't have been if she didn't know about the company. Aside from the hospital, it was basically the major employer in the area that, until Tristan established it, had been more traditionally comprised of primarily ranchers and farmers.

"We still have boxes to unpack in the bedrooms," she admitted. "But still, regardless of your family connection, it's a much too valuable gift for her. And I don't want her thinking that a person should be rewarded like that for trying to do a good deed."

No good deed goes unpunished, he thought cynically. "She'd have bought it herself at some store in Braden if she'd had enough money left from whatever it was she bought you."

Her lips twisted a little. "All right." Her voice lowered. "If you *must* know, I've already gotten her the game for her birthday."

"Then let her use the gift certificate on something else from CeeVid. If you want to take her over to them—you can't miss it. It's the multistory building out near the highway if you were heading to Braden. Anyway, she can shop for something on their Web site if you don't want to go to the store there. Consider it a birthday present if you have to, because I'm not taking it back."

She sighed hugely. "For crying in the sink," she muttered.

At the phrase, something inside Ryan's head clicked into place.

"You do want your way, don't you," Mallory was still muttering as she slipped past him into the hall.

"Cassie," he realized aloud. "That's who you remind me of. Cassie *Keegan*. Hell. You're related to her, aren't you? No wonder you seemed familiar."

Mallory went still at his words.

She'd come to Weaver for the express purpose of meeting Ryan Clay. She'd continually debated the decision until she'd convinced herself she was doing the right thing.

So why was she practically shaking in her boots now?

She'd never expected to meet him and feel anything… well…like what she was feeling.

The wrinkle in his forehead that had been there every time he looked at her was gone. "We worked together for a while. She didn't talk much about her family, though."

Ryan couldn't know that he'd just confirmed another

piece of the puzzle that had been her sister's life. "Cassie was my sister."

The wrinkle returned. In spades. "Was?"

She hesitated. The sound of the leaking water dripping into the bucket under the sink seemed loud. From downstairs, she could hear her grandmother and Chloe talking in the kitchen, along with the clatter of pots and the squeak of Kathleen's sturdy shoes on the creaking hardwood floor.

She also could hear in her head Ryan's mother's voice. And the pleas as well as the caution when it came to her son's state of mind. Rebecca Clay was desperate to help her son and believed that Mallory could help him find his path again. Rebecca had also gone to great lengths to assure Mallory that no matter what, her position as Chloe's mother would not be threatened in any way.

"Mallory," Ryan prompted.

She swallowed again. "I didn't expect this to be so hard," she admitted, as much to herself as to him. "Cassie…died."

He frowned. Muttered a soft oath. "On a case?"

"You mean work?" She shook her head, thinking of the strange company that her sister had worked for. And how difficult it had been to glean information from HW Industries about her sister and her coworkers. "No. She died in, um, in childbirth." Her mouth felt dry as she gave him the barest of explanations. "With Chloe."

His eyes were already a sharp blue. But his gaze went even sharper. "I thought you were her mother."

"I am." She picked at a loose thread on her sleeve. "Legally." Emotionally, too, which was something Mallory truly hadn't expected when everything she'd planned for her life had taken a ninety-degree turn courtesy of a four-pound, twelve-ounce infant. "But she's my niece by birth. She…well, Chloe knows Cassie was her birth mother. I've never kept that a secret from her."

"Her birthday is soon."

"Next Saturday," she confirmed.

"She's going to be seven?"

Her throat tightened even more. She nodded silently. Willing him to get to the finish line before she did, but afraid in a way, too, that he would.

"I worked with Cass nearly eight years go."

"I know." Her sleeve was beginning to unravel. She shoved the long thread up inside the knit and folded her hands together, only to pull them apart again. "She mentioned it." Only his first name, though, which had added to her challenge considerably.

He was watching her closely, his face oddly pale. "What else did she mention?"

The muscles in her abdomen were so tight they ached. "She said you...that you worked together once. That you were friends. And that you were a good man."

But his lips twisted at that. And his eyes were suddenly consumed by a hollowness that was painful to witness. "And did she tell you that we slept together, too?"

Lying was out of the question. "Yes."

Even beneath the dark, unshaven haze blurring his jaw, she could see a muscle flex there as he absorbed that. "Why, exactly, are you here in Weaver, Dr. Keegan?"

Mallory pulled in a steadying breath. He already knew. She could see it in his face.

But it had been a long haul for Mallory to reach this point. A journey that had taken years and more turns than she could have dreamed of.

She had to say the words.

She looked up at him. Meeting that shocked, hollow gaze with her own. "So that my daughter can meet her father."

Chapter Three

Even braced as Ryan thought he was, hearing Mallory's husky words was like taking a blow straight to the solar plexus. "No," he said flatly. "Can't be."

He and Cassie had slept together—what? A handful of times? His brain searched through memories. Sifting. Discarding.

Even less than a handful, he thought.

Twice.

The first time when she'd gotten his tail out of a sling by maintaining his cover that had been about to blow during an identity-theft sting, and the second time a few weeks later after they'd shared a few drinks following a debriefing they'd both attended.

"Obviously, without Cassie, I've had to speculate some," Mallory allowed. "But a test would confirm—"

"No," he said again. He stretched out his arm. Some portion of his mind recognized that he was backing away from her, as if to keep her and her impossible claim at bay. "I don't need any tests. I'm not—you don't want me to be her—" Christ. He couldn't even say it.

Her eyebrows were pulling together but the only thing he could see in her amber eyes was concern. And—oh, hell. Compassion.

He didn't want it. Didn't deserve it. "I've got to go." He turned on his heel and was halfway down the stairs before she could react.

"Ryan, wait. I'm not expecting anything. But please stay." Her shoes sounded on the stairs behind him. "Let's at least discuss it."

He passed Kathleen, who was holding a round tray filled with mugs, and Chloe, who was carrying a plate of Christmas-tree-green frosted cookies. He took in the details as he reached the door, even though their faces were almost a blur.

A second later he was outside. On the porch. Down the snow-covered walkway that bore dozens of footprints heading both to and from the house. This time, his were spaced more widely apart.

He knew he'd left his coat inside but he didn't hesitate. Just yanked open the squeaking door of the pickup truck and twisted the key that he'd left in the ignition. He gunned the engine and shot down the narrow street.

Yeah, he was running.

So what?

If the women in that house knew what he was—who he was—they'd thank him for it.

With only a bare regard for the stop sign at the corner, he turned at the end of the street. The Sleep Tite parking lot was half-full when he passed it. The parking lot lights that were draped with metal Christmas tree figures were just flicking on to glow against the lengthening afternoon.

He had no destination in mind, other than *away,* but when

he passed the hardware store, an oath blistered his tongue and he swung the truck around and parked it.

The Christmas shoppers were out in force. Even the aisles of the hardware store were crowded when he went inside. It was either the expression on his face or the purpose in his stride that fortunately kept the more familiar faces from trying to stop him to shoot the breeze. He found the repair clamps, bought a couple and headed back out to his truck.

"Ryan!"

He jerked to a stop, recognizing his father's voice even before he turned to see Sawyer Clay walking along the sidewalk, Ryan's mother on his arm.

Another downside of small-town living.

Running into people when you weren't prepared, every time you turned around.

"Dad. Mom," he greeted when they reached him.

"Where's your coat?" his mother asked, after she'd tugged his head down to plant a kiss on his cheek.

He had no intention of explaining that one, so he just held up the small plain brown paper sack from the hardware store. "Was just running in and out." It wasn't a lie, so meeting his gray-haired father's gaze wasn't entirely impossible. "What are you two doing in town?"

"What everyone else in town is doing," Sawyer drawled. "Taking their wives shopping. It's either Christmas presents or a dress for that shindig in a few weeks."

Rebecca made a face at him and batted his arm with her leather-gloved hand. "You *said* you wanted to come with me."

"Only to keep your spending in check." But there was a smile in his voice and an amused tick at the corner of his lips that belied his words. "Haven't seen you for a few days, son. How are things out at J.D.'s?"

J. D. Clay was his cousin whom he'd been helping out. Or maybe he should say that she was helping him out, by giving him something productive to fill the endless days. She'd moved back to Weaver a few months earlier and started up her own horse-boarding operation, and rather than stare endlessly at the walls of his motel room every day, he'd offered his assistance. So far, he'd begun repainting her old barn, fed and groomed horses and shoveled a mountain of horse manure out of their stalls. Tasks that were a million miles away from the career he'd left behind.

"Between Jake and his boys and Latitude's recovery, I've hardly seen her," he admitted. Latitude was an injured Thoroughbred that J.D.'s brand-new fiancé, Jake Forrest, had owned until he'd signed over ownership to her barely a week ago.

"Her shoulder is doing well," Rebecca inserted. She would know since not only was she still practicing, but she ran the hospital where J.D. had gone when she'd dislocated her shoulder after a tumble from a horse. "Doesn't hurt that she and Jake are clearly head-over-heels for each other." She dashed her hand over Ryan's shoulder. "Is everything all right? You look...distracted."

Distracted didn't begin to cover it. But talking about Mallory and her claim was the last thing he intended on doing.

"He's in a hurry, Bec," Sawyer inserted. "That's all." But Ryan still recognized the speculation in his father's eyes.

"Of course. We won't keep you out in the cold, sweetheart. But will we see you tomorrow for Sunday dinner? I'm on kitchen duty this time."

The Clay family members generally rotated around the big family meal every Sunday. Whoever could come did, and whoever couldn't, didn't.

But he'd made a point of avoiding the meals since his return to town.

And now, he could see the shadow of disappointment in his mother's eyes even before he'd formed an answer. From the corner of his eye, he could see the mechanical Santa positioned inside the front window of the hardware store waving merrily.

"Maybe," he said, instead of the refusal that was ready and waiting on his tongue.

She smiled, so clearly buoyed by a shot of hope, yet so clearly trying to contain it. "Well." She patted his shoulder again, then tucked her hands around Sawyer's arm. "You know where we'll be. Now go on before you catch your death of cold."

Like the solid unit that they'd been for most of his life, his parents stood close to each other, watching as he headed to his truck. When he got inside and tossed the paper sack on the seat beside him, they waved and smiled, and he lifted a hand before backing out of the parking space.

He drove back to Mallory's house only to sit, engine idling, at the curb. His hands clenched the steering wheel. He was looking at the house—two-storied, sharply gabled roof, narrow porch running across the entire front—but his thoughts were turned inward.

If Cassie had gotten pregnant, why hadn't she told him?

They'd both worked for Hollins-Winword, though she—an expert in foreign languages—had been in a support position to Coleman Black, rather than in the field like Ryan had been. Their paths had crossed occasionally. Never more closely than when she'd voluntarily interjected herself into that sting to save his bacon. She'd been smart and gutsy and engaging and he remembered genuinely enjoying her company, brief though it had been. And he was damn sure that her feelings toward him had been no more involved or deep. He hadn't loved her. She hadn't loved him.

He pinched the pain behind the bridge of his nose.

It was hard to believe she'd died bearing a child.

Not any child.

Chloe.

He jerked and started when someone knocked on the window beside him, and stifled a curse over his own edginess.

Mallory stood on the curb. This time, she was wearing a long, beige wool coat with a hood pulled over her head. She looked more like she belonged on the cover of a magazine than standing on the curb in little Weaver, Wyoming.

She was holding his leather coat.

"You came back," she said through the window. "I wasn't sure you would," she added, stepping away when he pushed open the door and got out.

He sorely wished he could just give her the paper sack with the repair clamps and be on his way, but some deeply buried streak inside him made him stay. "Does Chloe know? About…who…her father is?" It was a cowardly way of phrasing it. He knew it. She knew it.

But he gave Mallory credit for not pointing out that particular fact.

She just shook her head and held out his coat. "She doesn't know anything. And, to be honest, I prefer it that way. Until…until—" She broke off. A line of worry bisected the smooth skin between her eyebrows.

He dropped the paper bag on the hood of the truck and took the coat, pulling it on. "Until?"

She let out a soft, huffing breath that sent a vaporous cloud between them. "I'm sorry. I just don't know any good way of doing this," she admitted. "Telling you. Telling her. But Chloe's welfare is my primary concern. And if you…if you're not…well, if this is going to cause her any harm—" She shook her head, breaking off again. "I wish there was a manual for situations like this," she murmured.

"I doubt it would cover someone like me, anyway." He shoved his hand through his hair and was relieved that it wasn't shaking, because everything inside of him was feeling pretty damn unhinged. "Keep watching out for your daughter," he said abruptly. "That's what a good parent does."

She was nibbling at her lip and, despite everything, he got

distracted by their well-defined softness all over again. "Don't tell her," he added doggedly.

"Not yet," she clarified.

That wasn't the "not ever" that had been whispering through his brain. "Do you want support money or something?"

Her head reared back, the hood slipping off her shining hair. "That's what you think this is about? Money?"

He lifted his hand, peaceably. "I'm sorry." And he was. "I'm not trying to offend you. Just…to understand what it is that you do want."

The offended glint in her eyes slowly softened. She pushed her hands into the side pockets of her coat and rocked on her feet.

He immediately recognized the motion. Chloe had done the same exact thing in the diner.

"I want my daughter to know she has a father." Her gaze didn't meet his. Instead, it was focused somewhere off over his left shoulder.

"Lots of kids don't have a father around." Some were better off, too.

The corners of her lips curved downward. "Did you have *your* father around?"

He'd had two, actually. His mother, believing her relationship with Ryan's natural father was over, had married Tom Morehouse, who'd raised him until he'd died when Ryan was seven. A few years later his mom and Sawyer reconciled and had never been apart again. "Yeah. I did." He sighed. The paper sack crinkled as he held it up. "The repair clamp you need," he said. "I brought you a few extra."

She blinked a little, obviously surprised. "Thank you. I was going to run to the store before they closed, but—"

"Now you won't need to." He jerked his chin toward the house. "I'll put it on if you want."

"That's really not necessary," she demurred.

But he saw the hopefulness behind the words. "Might as

well." He wasn't opposed to offering the assistance. He just would have preferred to offer it to an absolute and utter stranger, instead of this woman with her impossibly sexy mouth and her claims about him and her daughter. "I'm here."

And they were evidently just one big, happy family.

Mallory wasn't ungrateful for the offer of assistance, but as she led the way up the sidewalk that she hadn't had time yet to shovel, she found herself wishing the assistance weren't coming from *him*.

She hadn't expected him to do cartwheels of joy when she'd told him about Chloe. She couldn't think of many men who would appreciate such news coming right out of the woodwork. And while she was trying to be fair—to see the situation from all sides—she didn't have a hope of really succeeding there, because she was firmly rooted on Chloe's side.

A child deserved to know their father. Period.

To this day, she still couldn't understand Cassie's decision not to tell Ryan about the baby at the time. Growing up, her older sister's life had been just as devoid of a father as Mallory's. Maybe Cassie would have changed her mind after Chloe was born if she'd lived to have the chance.

Unfortunately, that was something that Mallory simply would never know.

She preceded Ryan into the house and without a word, he practically bolted up the stairs the minute she'd pushed the door shut after them.

The sensible part of her told her to follow him and watch what he did with those clamp things so that she could do it herself the next time if she had to. But the rest of her mutinied and, instead, she dropped her coat on the hard-backed chair sitting in the front entry next to the narrow console table, and went into the kitchen where Chloe and Kathleen were.

Both were wearing Kathleen's hand-sewn aprons tied around their neck and waists and both of them were in flour up to their elbows as they kneaded bread dough on the counter. The only difference between them was that Kathleen was sitting on a bar stool while she worked, and Chloe was standing on a chair. Beyond that, their concentrated expressions were almost identical.

And neither seemed to have noticed the sound of Ryan in the house. She decided to leave it that way for now and stood silently in the doorway.

Just watching them eased nerves that were feeling slightly singed.

Are you seeing this, Cassie? Chloe's making rolls with Gram just the same way you and I used to.

"Get yourself an apron, Mallory," Kathleen said without looking. "There's another dough ball for you, too, if you want."

Mallory just smiled. She walked over behind the only people in the world that she would do anything for, and kissed first the top of Chloe's head, then Kathleen's papery-thin cheek. "I need to call the hospital and check on a patient." She also needed to deal with the very disturbing man upstairs repairing her plumbing.

"Work, work, work," Kathleen tsked, but without any real heat. "Just remember, there is more to life than work."

"Yes, Gram," she agreed dutifully, and just as dutifully admired Chloe's handiwork with the bread dough before escaping to her office at the back of the house.

She made her phone call to the hospital, talking briefly with the nurse on duty, but that didn't take long. Her new mom was recovering as nicely as expected.

Which left Mallory with nothing to do but go up the stairs.

She didn't find Ryan still in the bathroom, though. That small room was quite empty. She looked behind the cabinet door to see the pipe and its new clamp. There was no sign of water leaking, and the bucket she'd used was empty and sitting on the edge of the tub.

He'd even emptied the box containing the shampoos and soaps and whatnot that she'd pulled from the cabinet, replacing everything neatly inside it once more.

His thoroughness—his thoughtfulness—was disconcerting.

Was it possible that he could have left without her hearing his exit?

She slowly closed the cabinet and went out into the hall. Her bedroom was closest to the stairs. Chloe's was farthest. She turned in that direction and found Ryan there.

He was sitting on the foot of the twin-size bed looking very large and very masculine amid the lilac-hued, childish décor, and her footsteps faltered at the visceral tug the sight of him gave her deep inside.

"I'm getting the hint that she likes purple," he said after a moment.

She swallowed and managed a faint smile that hopefully masked the strange breathlessness she felt and stepped inside the room, leaning her shoulder back against the doorjamb. "It's been her favorite color since she discovered the Purple Princess games a few years ago from a school friend."

"What grade is she in?"

She discreetly hauled in a breath. Let it out. "Third."

His gaze finally slanted to hers. "Isn't she a little young for third?"

"She skipped second grade." She tugged at her ear. "I know that not everyone thinks that's a good idea, but she's so bright and I started her in second at the beginning of the school year when we were still in New York, but she was—"

"Bored," he inserted.

She looked at him a little more closely. It was hard, considering that doing so made her stomach flip around even more in those jittering circles.

But there wasn't judgment in his deeply blue eyes.

She wasn't sure exactly what *was* there, but at least she could tell that. "Yes. She was bored. She was bored through a good portion of the first grade, too." And bored schoolchildren tended to find more interesting things to keep them busy. Particularly mischievous things.

"I skipped third," he said.

"Oh." She moistened her lips.

"And ninth," he added without expression. "And most of my senior year of high school."

"That's…impressive."

His lips twisted a little. "You registered her over at the elementary school?"

"Yes." There wasn't an alternative, anyway. Weaver had one elementary school. One junior high. One high school. And unless it would have been on scholarship, she couldn't have afforded the tuition for private school even if there'd been one for Chloe to attend. Mallory's medical school hadn't come cheaply.

She would be paying off her student loans for some time to come.

"That's when the school and I decided to start her off here in third grade," she finished. "So far, she's keeping up with no problem at all."

"Sarah Scalise her teacher?"

Was Weaver so small that a single man with no children would know that? Her mind veered off much too easily. Maybe he'd even dated the attractive teacher. "Yes."

"She's my cousin."

She was appalled at the relief that flooded through her. Her interest in the man was supposed to be only because of Chloe. Not…not—

"What are your plans tomorrow?"

Her runaway thoughts screeched to a halt. "Um, nothing much. More unpacking. And Chloe is becoming anxious that we won't ever get around to getting a Christmas tree, so I imagine I'll have to find a tree lot somewhere."

"Folks around here cut their own trees," he said.

Her lips parted, dismayed. "Like with a saw?"

His blue eyes suddenly lit with amusement, and years seemed to fall away from his face. "That's the usual method," he said, only slightly tongue-in-cheek.

Safely hidden behind her back, Mallory's hands curled. She smiled weakly.

The corner of his lips lifted a little more. The flash of white teeth was brief, but it was still there, when he actually smiled. "Never cut a Christmas tree yourself?"

"Right up there with fixing plumbing leaks, I'm afraid."

He pushed off the bed and walked toward her. Her spine pressed hard against the doorjamb as she looked up at him when he stopped next to her.

There was plenty of space between them, but her heart rate nevertheless took off like an award-winning marathoner. The only time she'd felt anything remotely similar was the first time she'd delivered a baby. Not even with Brent, her one foray into romance while she'd been a resident, had she been so affected.

His gaze roved over her face and she swallowed hard, afraid he'd hear the pulse roaring in her ears.

"I'll pick you and Chloe up at noon," he said, and the amusement was gone from his face as if it had never been there. "That oughta give us plenty of time."

"Time," she repeated faintly.

"To find you a tree," he said flatly, and walked out into the hall. He didn't look back.

For so long, Mallory had been certain that finding Chloe's father was the right thing to do.

But just then, watching Ryan head down the stairs as if the devil were at his heels, she realized she wasn't certain of anything.

Chapter Four

He was twenty minutes late.

So far.

Twenty minutes during which Chloe paced between the windows at the front of the house, pressing her nose against the glass, as she watched and waited. "Are you *sure* he's coming?"

Mallory's gaze snagged in Kathleen's, who was sitting opposite her, before she looked back down at the medical journal lying open in her lap. Reading it was just a pretense, because Mallory could have easily emulated Chloe's anxious pacing, waiting for Ryan's arrival.

"If he doesn't," she assured smoothly, "we'll just get a Christmas tree ourselves." Maybe there was a tree lot in Braden. The neighboring town was about thirty miles away. Certainly there'd be one in Gillette—though she really didn't relish the idea of driving quite that far.

The solution, of course, would be an artificial tree, purchased from the discount store on the outskirts of town.

Only Mallory knew that both Chloe and Kathleen would be disappointed. They'd been talking about having a *real* tree ever since they'd arrived in Weaver. Even when they'd left New York in October, the Christmas decorations had begun appearing in stores. There was barely a fraction of the stores in Weaver, but they, too, had already been getting ready for the holidays.

"Can we get a puppy, too?" Chloe asked, without looking away from the window.

Mallory met Kathleen's eyes. "No," she answered. "We're not getting a puppy."

Chloe heaved a sigh. "Do you think we'll find a really, really big tree?"

If he gets here, Mallory thought.

"He'll be here," Kathleen said comfortably over the soft clack of her knitting needles. "And I'm sure you'll find a very fine tree."

Mallory had the sense that her grandmother was assuring *her* just as much as Chloe.

She realized she was chewing the inside of her lip and made herself stop. Folding the journal with a snap, she tossed it aside and pushed off the couch, taking her half-empty coffee mug with her. Another ten minutes, and she'd bundle Chloe in the car and they'd drive to Braden. Kathleen had already expressed her intention to enjoy the tree once it was in the living room. Hunting one down whether in the snow or from a tree lot was not something she particularly wanted to do.

"He's here!" Chloe suddenly darted past Mallory, her boots skidding on the floor as she raced out of the living room to the front door.

Mallory ignored both the jolt that leaped inside her belly *and* the sideways glance that Kathleen gave her—as if her grandmother knew exactly what Mallory was feeling—and followed her daughter much more sedately to the door.

When she got there, Chloe had already thrown it wide and

Ryan stood there on the porch, looking almost unrecognizable with his clean-shaven square jaw. Even his hair looked different. Not cut, necessarily, but brushed away from his face, showing that there was a liberal amount of silver strands among the dark brown.

The severe style made his eyes seem an even deeper, more penetrating blue, and when their focus shifted upward from Chloe to Mallory, every single coherent thought she possessed disappeared in a puff of smoke.

She felt as though he had the ability to look straight down inside her. And was using the ability very well.

It felt…invasive.

Intimate.

She realized belatedly that Chloe was tugging at the hem of her sweater, and she finally yanked her captured gaze away from him. She looked at Chloe, but her brain cells were sluggish. "What is it, sweetheart?"

Chloe's eyebrows were crinkled. "You're spilling," she whispered.

Mallory jerked a little, flushing hard. Along with coherent thought, her hands had gone as lax as her knees had felt, the coffee mug sliding sideways in her fingers. "Silly me," she murmured, excessively bright.

She grabbed the closest cloth—her red knitted scarf that was hanging over the coat tree—and dashed it over the small spill on the floor. "I'll be right back." She couldn't prevent herself from flicking a glance toward Ryan, then wished she hadn't, because he was still watching her.

The day before, he'd been a handsome—albeit very scruffy-looking—man.

With his strong features no longer hidden behind too-long, unkempt hair, and a bristled jaw that had been somewhere between a beard and a thirteen-o'clock shadow, he seemed positively devastating.

She felt so rattled that instead of putting the mug in the kitchen where it belonged—and where she'd intended to take it in the first place—she carried it and the red scarf with her upstairs and closed herself in her bedroom.

The mug bobbled sideways when she dumped it on her dresser and she steadied it with a very unsteady hand. The wide mirror hanging on the wall above the dresser reflected most of the bedroom behind her. But she didn't see the stack of packing cartons in the corner next to the sleigh bed that she'd found years ago in a junk store and refinished with Kathleen's help.

What she did see were her own eyes staring back at her. Pupils wide, irises a thin brown. So very different from those deeply penetrating blue ones that consumed her mind's eye.

What had he seen when he'd looked at her?

Who had he seen? Mallory, or Cassie?

Mallory closed her eyes, turning away from the mirror and the thought. She wasn't in competition with her beloved sister. She was only trying to make sure that Chloe's life had what hers and Cassie's had lacked.

A father.

She yanked off the ivory sweater that she'd taken far too long to choose that morning in the first place and replaced it with a gray one, yanking it down over the waist of her blue jeans. In the connecting bathroom, she filled the sink and submerged the coffee-stained scarf in it. Mentally collecting herself seemed fine in theory, but sad to say, she still felt shaky when she went back downstairs.

Kathleen was standing alone in the foyer.

"Where's Chloe?"

"Outside with Ryan." Her grandmother's expression was frank. "Are you certain you know what you're getting into, Mallory?"

She crossed her arms. Fighting her own uncertainty was hard enough without adding her grandmother's into the mix. "In life, can anyone ever really know what they're getting into?"

Kathleen's lips thinned. "Pretending to wax philosophical won't wash with me, child." She pointed at the closed front door. "You're messing in a lot of lives because of this fixation you've got about Chloe and her father."

"It's not a fixation."

Kathleen's white eyebrows climbed. Ire filled her eyes. "Really, now. It's been your obsession since Chloe was born. When you should have been finding a man of your own, you were focused only on *him*."

"I'm a working single mother," Mallory returned. "I've never had *time* for a man." Ergo, the exit of Brent. The fact that she hadn't been left brokenhearted at the time had seemed to prove that it had been for the best. She'd never been tempted to put a man before her career. "And we've talked about this many times." She'd never made a secret with her grandmother about the reason behind their temporary transplant to Weaver.

"Aye. We have. Yet you're still determined to do it your way."

"If I had *my* way, Cassie would still be here," Mallory pointed out, struck with pain that was only slightly dulled by the passage of time. "Raising the child she loved enough to die having." But, of course, Cassie—adventurous, go-with-the-moment Cassie—hadn't believed she'd ever face that most final result despite Mallory's warnings. "And choosing what to do about Chloe's father would have been *her* decision."

"She made the decision," Kathleen reminded. Her face had softened, but her voice was still firm. "She had nearly the entire duration of her pregnancy to contact him. She *chose* not to."

"I believe she would have changed her mind." And arguing

the point with her grandmother was as fruitless as the internal debate that had gone on for years inside Mallory about that very point.

She grabbed her coat off the coat tree and shoved her arms into the sleeves. "You seemed to like Ryan just fine, yesterday when he was here. So what's bothering you about him now, anyway?"

"It's not *me* that he's bothering," Kathleen said pointedly.

Mallory focused on working her hands into the gloves she pulled out of her coat pockets and tried not to blush. "All I care about is Chloe. Once I'm certain she's ready for it, I'll tell her about him and we'll take it from there."

"Right. And then it'll be time for us to go back to New York. And how do you think Chloe's going to handle being taken away from the father she's just met, then?"

It wasn't a new concern, nor was it one that Mallory hadn't already given plenty of thought to. "She'll still be able to talk to him. To see him during school breaks." She pushed her pager and her cell phone into the breast pocket of the wool coat. "I knew before we got here that if…everything worked out…it would ultimately mean coming up with some sort of visitation agreement." She reached for the door.

"What if *you're* the one who ends up on the visiting side?"

"That's not going to happen," she said surely, and pulled open the door.

Ryan and Chloe were bent over an enormous snowball, pushing it together across the yard. The expressions of concentration on their faces were nearly identical.

Mallory swallowed the unease that whispered through her and stepped outside. Chloe had on her coat, her mittens, a scarf and a cap that Kathleen had knitted for her. Usually, she managed to forget the scarf or the hat. "Gram's going to be popping the corn soon for garland," she called out to them, "so we'd better come back with a worthy tree."

Ryan looked over his shoulder. His head was bare. He wore no scarf tucked around his neck. His only concessions to the cold were the gloves on his hands and the scarred-up leather jacket zipped halfway up his chest. "Popcorn garland?"

Chloe straightened away from the snowball that was easily as tall as her knees and held her hands wide as she bounced around, full of energy. "We use Grammy's needles on *long* string. It's fun."

Ryan continued pushing the snowball toward the house. "If you say so. Where do you want your snowman, Chloe?"

"Right *here*." Chloe dashed over to a spot near the steps. "I asked him if he'd ever made one and he said he did, and so we're getting one now," she provided needlessly. "I never had a snowman before." She beamed at Ryan when he nudged the ball to a stop. "Can I have a carrot for his nose?"

The delight in Chloe's expression would have been impossible to resist, even had Mallory wanted to. "I imagine we have a carrot to spare," she assured. "But your snowman still needs a little more body before he needs a nose, doesn't he?"

"Yeah." Ryan scooped up a large handful of snow before straightening, and packed it between his gloved palms until it was the size of a healthy grapefruit. "Might as well finish it now, kiddo." He cast an eye toward the sky. "It's going to be snowing by the end of today—tomorrow at the latest— judging by the sky and then it might be a while before the snow is wet enough again to pack well."

"What about the tree?"

His gaze skated over Mallory, leaving heat in its wake. "We'll get to it. Here." He tossed the snowball toward her and she didn't react quickly enough to catch it.

It landed harmlessly against her chest and burst into a spray of clumps.

"Mo-om," Chloe groaned. "You were s'posed to catch it."

"Sorry." Mallory went down the steps and scooped up her

own snowball. She eyed Ryan, speculatively. He was a perfect target, leaning over, gathering up another handful of snow.

"Wouldn't try it, Doc," he warned, without looking at her.

She tossed the snowball from one hand to the other. "Try what?"

He straightened and gave her a glance that succeeded in making her mouth feel parched. It also made a mockery of her innocent claim. "Here." He handed his latest snowball off to Chloe. "You can do this one on your own. It's going to be the head, so it doesn't have to be as large as the base."

Chloe knelt down and began scooping snow around her assignment. The tip of her tongue peeked out from between the corner of her lips.

Before Mallory even knew he'd moved, Ryan plucked the snowball from her hands. "I'll take that," he said, and began adding to it.

Within minutes, both he and Chloe were rolling their snowballs across the yard and right into the neighbor's property, picking up snow as they went. Mallory smoothed her coat beneath her and sat down on the porch steps, watching.

But Chloe wasn't having any of that. "Mom, you gotta help!"

So Mallory dutifully rose again and walked over to her daughter.

"Not me," Chloe said. "Him." She waved toward Ryan, who, in Mallory's estimation, needed no assistance whatsoever with maneuvering his snowman-middle even if it were already twice the size of Chloe's somewhat sausage-shaped head.

It was only the flash of amusement she caught on Ryan's face—as if he fully expected her to refuse—that made Mallory move over beside him and plant her hands next to his on the snowball. "For someone who didn't seem very enthusiastic about today," she said under her breath, "you seem to be ending up quite entertained."

"And we haven't even left your neighborhood, yet." His

hands steered the snowball toward the left, circling back in the direction of her house and the snowman's base.

"Are we really going to find a Christmas tree today?"

"I said we would." His shoulder brushed against hers. "When I say I'll do something, I'll do it."

"Even if you didn't want to," she concluded, her voice just as low.

His jaw tightened. He stopped pushing the snowball, which was easily the size of three watermelons. "What do you want from me?"

She looked at him. The answer should have been so easy. A father for Chloe. Better yet, an…interested and caring father for Chloe.

So why wasn't it easy?

"Mom. Mr. Ryan. Look at my head!" Chloe stood over her lopsided snowball with pride. "Is it big enough?"

"Looks great," Ryan answered. He rolled the snowball he and Mallory had formed the last few yards, then picked it up and settled it on the base before adding Chloe's to the top. "There you go, kiddo. Your first snowman," he told Chloe.

"I wanna get his face now," Chloe said, dashing up the stairs and disappearing through the front door that she threw open.

"If I hadn't wanted to take you out to find a tree, I wouldn't have offered in the first place," he told Mallory the second Chloe was out of earshot.

She shoved her hands inside the side pockets of her coat, hiding the fists they had curled into. "Then why did you tear out of here yesterday the way that you did after offering?" Her voice had risen, and she swallowed, looking around.

But Chloe hadn't come back outside, and the houses flanking hers were as still and silent as they'd been since Mallory had come outside.

The only one around listening to them was the faceless, limbless snowman.

She sighed and pulled her hands out of her pockets again. "Look. I know I dropped a bombshell on you yesterday. Of course it's going to take some time for you—for all of us—to adjust to that. But—"

"It's not Chloe that bothers me." He grimaced. "Well, yeah, but not in the way that you probably mean," he amended.

"I don't understand."

"I know." He looked at her, only this time his focus was turned inward. "And it's not something I'm going to explain."

His choice of words caught her. He wouldn't explain. Not *couldn't*. Not *shouldn't*.

"I got his face stuff." Chloe reappeared and the door slammed behind her, sounding as loud as a gunshot. She was clutching a handful of items against her coat. "Grammy said we could use these cookies for his eyes." She dropped the rest of her collection onto the snow next to the snowman, and held up two round, chocolate-flavored cookies. "I guess I want him to have eyes more 'n I want to eat them," she admitted with a giggle. "Here. Put 'em on."

Ryan nearly winced. Chloe was holding the cookies toward him with such trusting faith in her face that it was painful.

Mallory didn't say anything. Just continued watching him with an expression that seemed to ride the rails between caution and expectation, hope and compassion.

He wanted to tell her not to expect anything. Not from him. It would be safer all the way around.

But he couldn't make himself do it.

And he was damned if he knew whether that was because he didn't want to see the disappointment in her eyes the same way he saw disappointment in the eyes of his family, or if it was because he, himself, didn't want to feel the loss when that disappointment inevitably occurred.

Instead of taking the cookies from Chloe, he simply went

over behind her and lifted her up by the waist so she could reach the snowman's head. "Give the poor guy some eyes," he told her.

She giggled again and worked the cookies into the snow. "What's his name?"

"He's your snowman," Ryan reminded. "Think that gives you naming rights."

"I don't know no snowman names, though, except Frosty." She craned her head around to look up at Ryan. "Everyone names their snowman Frosty."

Mallory picked up the carrot and handed it to Chloe. "You don't know *any* snowman names," she corrected. "And yes, you do. Use your imagination." She shrugged. "Besides. Maybe your snowman is actually a woman. Have you thought about that?"

Chloe screwed the root end of the carrot into the snow. "Nope," she said surely. "He's a *snowman*."

Ryan wondered how she made the determination, but figured he was better off not knowing the finer points of how a six-year-old came to such a conclusion. He tipped her almost upside down so she could reach her pile on the ground and she squealed with laughter that didn't stop even when he turned her upright, again.

"Didja see that, Mom?" Chloe's feet swung freely, nearly knocking him in the knees and he swung her to his side, holding her against his hip.

"I saw," Mallory assured. "Are those candy canes for his mouth?"

"Yup." Chloe reached forward and methodically placed the two red-and-white candies. In Ryan's opinion, the resulting smile was maniacally cheerful, but Chloe was satisfied. And Mallory was watching her daughter with an indulgent smile.

"Okay, put me down." Chloe wriggled and he set her on her feet, only to nearly jump out of his skin when she slid her small hand, mitten and all, into his. "Come here, Mom," she beckoned. "I know his name."

Mallory joined them, taking Chloe's other hand as they faced the snowman.

"His name is George," Chloe announced with great seriousness. "George the Great."

George the fat, Ryan renamed silently, for the snowman was seriously rotund.

"Look this way and smile." Kathleen's voice sounded from behind them and he looked over his shoulder.

She was holding a camera to her face.

"Gram," Mallory protested.

"What? The best way to enjoy a snowman is in pictures," the woman said as the shutter busily clicked several times. Then she lowered the camera. "Seeing as how they tend to melt," she added, winking at Chloe.

"You're welcome to come with us," Ryan found himself offering. "There's room in the truck and we'll be back before dark."

"No, no. You go on."

"Are you sure?" Mallory added.

"As sure as I am old," Kathleen said wryly, and tucked the camera in the front pocket of the apron that wasn't completely covered by the shawl tossed around her shoulders.

"But you're making the popcorn, right?" Chloe let go of their hands and darted up the stairs to wrap her arms around her great-grandmother's waist. "Lots and lots so we'll have garland to string everywhere?"

"Absolutely." Kathleen squeezed Chloe's chin and backed up through the door again into the house. "But only if you get yourselves going."

"Call if you need anything," Mallory reminded. "If the cell doesn't go through, page me."

Kathleen just waved and closed the door, a smile on her face.

Now that the snowman was faced and named, Chloe wasted no time in switching her interest to the original goal of the day. "How long will it take to get a tree?"

"Longer, the more we stand around talking about it." He gestured toward his truck, parked at the curb. "It's unlocked."

She needed no other encouragement and her green boots flashed as she ran toward the truck. With a little finagling, she managed to get her foot up onto the running board and tugged open the door. A second later, she disappeared inside.

Ryan looked at Mallory and extended his arm. "After you."

She took a few, halting steps toward the truck. "Not to sound like Chloe, but how long *is* this likely to take? I have a patient at the hospital I need to see by this evening, so if the tree farm is really out of the way—"

"There's no tree farm," he cut in.

Her feet stopped altogether "But I thought you said we were going to cut one."

"We are. But not at a Christmas tree farm." In this neck of the woods, the idea was practically laughable.

"Then where?"

He exhaled. "In the woods behind my parents' place," he said, naming the best spot within miles. Nearly everyone in the family found their trees there. "It'll mean one catch, though."

"What?"

"Sunday dinner. With them."

Alarm filled her face. "With your parents?" She shot a glance at the truck and Chloe. "But—"

"Don't worry." His voice was short. "They don't know anything about her. I'm not likely to tell them about her when we're not even telling Chloe." He closed his hand around her elbow. He hadn't even warned his parents that he'd be bringing guests. That wouldn't be any more of a surprise or shock than *his* presence would be.

"But that's just it, Ryan." She still didn't move.

He didn't like the suspicion sinking through him like a rock. "*What* is just it?"

She moistened her lips, looking pained. "They *do* know about Chloe. At least your mother does. She has for a, um, a while."

He stared at her. "You want to tell me what the bloody *hell* you are talking about? How long a while?"

She glanced toward the truck. "Chloe's waiting. Maybe we should get into this later."

"There is no later," he said flatly. "Later involves dinner with my parents. Who apparently know things about me even when I don't."

"Don't be angry. There's a logical explanation."

"Mr. Ryan!" Chloe called from the truck. "Aren't we gonna go yet? I can't wait to see our Christmas tree!"

He exhaled roughly and shoved his hand through his hair. "Yeah," he answered her. But his focus was on Mallory. "I can't wait, either."

Chapter Five

The tree, when they found it, was indeed "really, really big." In fact, it was so wide and so tall that it barely seemed to fit in the bed of Ryan's pickup truck.

If Mallory hadn't been so unaccountably nervous about Ryan and his parents, she would have enjoyed the outing as thoroughly as Chloe had.

When he'd said the woods were behind his parents' home, she'd envisioned an acre or maybe two studded with trees behind a house.

Well, she hadn't even seen a house at all as Ryan had driven the truck off a paved and snowplowed road, onto a gravel, slush-covered one until even that seemed to end, and he'd parked, and told them they'd be going on foot from there.

Then he'd looped a coil of rope from his truck bed over one shoulder, hefted a chainsaw with his other hand, and led the way into the trees. "Stay close," he'd warned. "Don't lose sight of me."

She'd rapidly seen the value in that and had kept Chloe's hand tucked in hers as they carefully tramped through the woods where there'd been surprisingly little snow on the ground. Or not so surprising at all, she'd supposed, given how there was barely any sunlight filtering through the branches that grew overhead and all around.

They'd walked for maybe a half hour before the immense trees had thinned slightly and Ryan gestured at the fir trees surrounding them. "Take your pick."

Chloe had been agog at the choices and even though she'd picked one of the seemingly smaller trees, Mallory was still stunned at how very large it turned out to be.

And how little effort Ryan had seemed to expend in not only cutting and hauling it, but also tossing it into the truck bed afterward.

"It's going to be the bestest tree we've ever had," Chloe said for about the tenth time.

Foregoing the narrow rear seat, she was instead sitting on the bench seat between Mallory and Ryan, and even fastened securely into a seat belt, she still seemed able to bounce. "You're going to help decorate it, right?" She was talking to Ryan, and Mallory couldn't fail to miss the tormented look that flashed across his face. It was brief. But it was most definitely there.

"We'll see," he said.

Which most definitely wasn't an agreement—one of those things that if he said he'd do, he'd do.

Mallory looked away, staring blindly out the side window as the slushy gravel spit from beneath the tires and the truck rocked wildly.

Chloe was busy peppering him for details about how many Christmas trees he'd cut like this, and wasn't this particular one his most favorite? But Mallory's thoughts were too busy, too disturbing, to listen very closely.

She wished she'd have just told Ryan the entire story from

the first. Or better yet, that she'd have contacted him directly when she'd run into Rebecca at that medical conference just a few months earlier. Instead, she'd been so shocked to learn the man was actually alive that she'd been incapable of making any sort of immediate decision. It had been Rebecca who'd approached her to bring Chloe to Wyoming.

That Ryan needed something in his life other than fixing his cousin's barn up for her—and his mother believed the revelation of a daughter he'd never known existed would be that something.

She pressed her fingertips to her throbbing forehead only to realize that her pager was vibrating, too. She sighed a little and pulled it from her pocket, reading the display.

Both Ryan and Chloe were looking at her when she pocketed it once more. "The hospital," she said. "There's a case coming into the E.R. that they need me for. I'm afraid I'm going to have to cut this short, after all."

Chloe's face fell. Ryan looked…well, his expression didn't reveal a single thing. "I'll drive you there now," he said.

It was the most expedient way, of course, as opposed to taking her home first and then having to drive to the hospital, but she still found herself wanting to refuse. "Chloe—"

"I'll take her home after I drop you off." His gaze met hers over the little girl's head. "Your home," he added, obviously reading her mind.

Torn between gratitude and wariness, she finally nodded. "Thank you."

"But when are we gonna decorate the tree?"

Mallory ran her hand down Chloe's tumbled hair. "You and Gram can start on the garland without me. And I'll be there as soon as I can."

Chloe made a face. "I *hate* the hospital," she grumbled.

"Chloe," Mallory tsked softly. "The people I work with don't choose to make you or me unhappy."

But her daughter didn't lose her gloomy expression.

"I hated the hospital sometimes, too," Ryan said after a moment. He turned onto the paved road and the ride immediately grew smoother. "My mom worked there when I was a kid."

Grumbles abruptly forgotten, Chloe looked at him. She was obviously fascinated.

Mallory wished that her daughter was the only one.

Unfortunately, that wasn't the case and she found herself watching his profile as he spoke.

"She got called out at some of the worst times," he recounted. "Like when she was supposed to talk to my class during parent's day and Lea Rasmussen got to take my spot, instead and brought in hamburgers from her dad's restaurant. Hamburgers were a lot more interesting than tongue depressors."

"Mom was my show-and-tell last year," Chloe provided. "But she didn't have to leave. We made a poster board with pictures of the babies she helped deliver and hung it up on the bulletin board in my class." She leaned closer to Ryan. "There was a lot of pictures," she added in a loud whisper. "She put mine in the very center, but nobody knew it was me except for us."

Ryan looked across at her. "You delivered Chloe, too?"

"I was doing my residency. And yes, I was there when she was born." She could see the questions in his eyes. Questions she didn't particularly want to address, even if Chloe weren't sitting between them with her avid attention to details.

She kept to the subject of Chloe.

"She was a perfectly beautiful baby and she screamed from the moment her lungs filled with air. She also had a head as bald as a cue ball that stayed that way until she was nearly two years old." Smiling, she gently tugged Chloe's thick hair. Once her wispy-fine baby hair had begun thickening, it'd been a challenge keeping up with the thick, glossy strands that replaced it.

Chloe lifted the ends of her hair. "But I don't got curls like you," she said with a deep sigh, seemingly unaware of the elephant that had joined them in that cozy cab. The one there to remind her and Ryan of the obvious. With the exception of his silver streaks, Chloe's hair was pretty much the exact shade of Ryan's, right down to the walnut-brown gloss it had in the sunlight.

Ryan's gaze met hers over her daughter's head for a moment before he looked back at the road and turned the corner that would take them to the small hospital.

There was still a visible strain in his expression and she blamed it on the doctor in her that wanted to help.

If only she knew how. She couldn't very well take back Chloe's existence and, from what Mallory could tell, it was her little girl that disturbed Ryan. Whether he admitted it, or not.

"Which door? Main or E.R.?"

She dragged her thoughts back to where they belonged. "E.R., please."

With obvious familiarity, he drove around to the emergency room entrance and pulled to a stop in front of the doors right in the area reserved for ambulances.

Mallory slid out of the truck but leaned back in to kiss Chloe's cheek. "Behave for Grammy," she reminded. Needlessly, because Chloe was almost always very well behaved. "And don't forget to thank Mr. Clay for helping us find a tree," she added softly, though she could see that Ryan heard anyway.

She straightened and pushed the door closed, hesitating for a fraction of a second before turning to hurry into the emergency room.

But she'd stood there long enough to see the forced smile Ryan gave Chloe as he steered his truck away from the curb.

She was very much afraid that her desire to erase whatever torment he was carrying inside had little to do with her being a doctor.

And everything to do with being a woman.

"Dr. Keegan." Courtney Clay—Ryan's sister—was the nurse on duty at the desk. "Dr. Clay is waiting for you in surgery." Of course she was referring to her mother, Rebecca.

"Thanks." Feeling surrounded by Ryan's family at every turn, Mallory quickly headed through the double doors leading to the examining rooms and the corridor beyond. She stopped off in the locker room to twist her hair back into a ponytail, wash up and change into a pair of drab green scrubs and then elbowed through another doorway to the scrub sinks.

Above them was a window that overlooked the two operating rooms that the hospital possessed. In one, she could see the E.R.-dedicated physician, Dr. Jackman, and his staff laboring over a heart patient. In the other, she could see Rebecca Clay directing another team in their setup for the obstetric patient who had not yet arrived.

When Mallory was scrubbed in, capped, masked and gowned with the assistance of one of the technicians, she joined Rebecca. They'd barely had time to discuss the case coming in when the near-term patient arrived. And then there was no room for thinking about anything but saving not only the life of the critically ill mother, but the distressed baby as well.

The entire team worked quickly, efficiently, and with every speck of the skill Mallory had been accustomed to in New York. Rebecca took charge of the infant the moment he was delivered. Mallory continued her work with the mother and it was only afterward, when the patients—both of them—were transported to recovery with every expectation of a long future and Mallory had spoken with the woman's understandably frantic husband in the waiting room, that the stuffing finally went out of her legs.

She returned to the empty locker room, where she sank down on the hard bench between two short rows of lockers and peeled the ponytail holder from her hair, raking her fingers through the sweaty strands.

She'd shower and dress again and look in on Mrs. Olsen, her cesarean from the day before, and then figure out a way to get home.

She'd call Gram to come pick her up if she had to, but the day had already dwindled away until it was evening and it was near Chloe's bedtime. It'd be easier if she could bum a ride from one of the nurses going off shift.

"Good work in there today." Rebecca entered the small room and headed straight for a locker at the end of the row. She, too, still wore her scrubs, and she slipped the long white lab coat she pulled from a locker on over them. "I wasn't sure for a while there if we were going to be able to save them both."

"We were lucky," she murmured.

"Rhonda Danson and her baby were lucky to have you in there," Rebecca countered. "Your administrators in New York weren't exaggerating when they sang your praises. Weaver is benefitting a lot from your presence here." She closed her locker and leaned back against it. "How is…your family?"

Mallory looked down at the palms of her hands. Rebecca Clay was a beautiful woman who didn't look anywhere near old enough to have a son Ryan's age. And she was being inordinately tactful in her references to Chloe, whom they both knew was her granddaughter.

"Chloe's fine." She bit her lip and looked up at the woman who'd exhibited nothing but kindness toward her, even before she'd ever seen Chloe. "She met Ryan yesterday, at Ruby's," she offered bluntly. "Since then, we, um, he's been spending some time with her."

Mallory had to give the woman credit. Rebecca looked shocked but managed to contain it well. "Yesterday," she repeated faintly. "I…see."

"I told him about Cassie and he seems to believe she's his—"

"Of course he believes it," Rebecca inserted with some spirit. "She's a miniature, female version of him."

There was no denying that. It was seeing Chloe with her own eyes that had made Rebecca realize what was behind Mallory's interest in locating her son. "Anyway, when we were out cutting a Christmas tree today, I'm afraid I had to tell him that you already knew about Chloe when he wanted us all to go to your house for Sunday dinner."

"Ah." Rebecca absorbed that. Her throat worked for a moment before she spoke again. "He was going to bring you for dinner."

Mallory nodded. "Of course that was before I was paged." Her hands spread. "And you obviously weren't there doing any cooking, either. I hope nobody had to go hungry as a result."

The older woman looked bemused. "There're enough able-bodied cooks to fill in for me. And produce much more appetizing results." A faint smile touched her lips. "To be honest, I don't know which surprises me more. The dinner part or the Christmas tree part. But it proves what I'd hoped. That Ryan would be unable to resist Chloe once he met her." She moved suddenly and sat down beside Mallory, closing her cool hands over Mallory's. "I don't know how to thank you enough," she said quietly. "You don't know what you're bringing back to my family."

The truth was, Mallory wasn't sure she knew what she was doing at all. Particularly with the tormented expression that Ryan carried much too often haunting her mind. "I'm not telling Chloe, yet," she admitted. Or maybe warned.

But that didn't seem to shock Rebecca at all. "You're her mother. You'll know when the time is right. Regardless of what anyone says, it *is* your decision."

"And Ryan's," Mallory felt compelled to add.

Rebecca's gaze was steady and thoughtful. "Yes. And Ryan's." She squeezed Mallory's hands again before pushing to her feet. "Are you heading out now?"

Mallory stood, also. "I promised to look in on Mrs. Olsen this evening. Then I'll find some way home." She turned to her locker and pulled out a clean towel. "I don't have my car with me because Ryan dropped me off."

"I'll give you a ride," Rebecca offered immediately. "Will an hour do? I'll meet you outside."

"I wasn't hinting—"

"I know." She headed toward the door, sending back a little smile as she pulled it open. "This is what family is for, my dear."

Mallory clutched her towel, watching the door swing shut after Ryan's mother.

Mallory had family. Even though she'd had no father, she'd had a mother until she'd been taken by breast cancer much too early. And after that, she'd had Gram. She had Chloe.

But she couldn't help the warmth she felt knowing that there were other people who cared, too. It might be only because of Chloe, but it still felt good.

That sense carried her right on through her visit with Mrs. Olsen, who was nursing her newborn and looking well. The only reason Mallory decided not to release her until morning was to give her another night of relatively peaceful sleep before she returned to her much more lively home and the demands of the two young children she and her husband already had.

But when she went out to the parking lot, it wasn't Rebecca Clay who was waiting for her.

It was Ryan.

He was sitting in his truck, parked beneath one of the tall lights that illuminated the modest-sized parking lot and was obviously watching for her, because the moment the hospital doors slid shut with a soft whoosh after her, he got out and stood by the side of his truck.

That oddly congested feeling climbed in her chest again, making it hard to breathe in any sort of normal fashion.

She was much more comfortable in her scrubs, dealing

with some emergency, than she was dealing with the uncertainty she felt every time she saw him.

Blowing out a breath, she held the collar of her coat more closely around her neck and crossed the parking lot toward him. "Your mother's giving me a ride," she greeted.

He pushed away from his slouch against the truck. "I saw her a few minutes ago. Told her I'd take care of it."

She'd have felt a lot safer with his mother. "I really didn't want to put either one of you out. I could have called Gram—"

"Chloe's already in bed." He cut her off, confirming what Mallory had expected in the first place.

But the fact that *he* knew that Chloe was in bed did surprise her.

"Once I managed to wrestle the tree into a stand and into your living room—it takes up half the room, by the way—I strung popcorn garland with them until she was practically falling asleep over the popcorn bowl," he said.

Something inside her melted at the image that immediately bloomed inside her mind. "How do you do that?" she asked. "Read my mind the way you do?"

"It's not difficult." He walked around the front of the truck with her and opened the passenger door for her. Then he took her arm and helped her up to the running board, and inside. "Everything you think or feel shows as plain as day in your eyes."

She hesitated and looked at him. The advantage of the seat's height put her head almost at the same level as his. "I'm not sure I like the idea of that."

A wisp of a smile drifted over his lips and her gaze dropped to them and clung. They were fuller than she'd realized.

Which was a realization she should *not* be having.

She carefully kept her eyes averted and settled more squarely in the seat. But when she blindly reached for the seat belt behind her right shoulder, her hand knocked into Ryan's and her gaze flew up to his all over again.

His thick lashes dropped slightly but she could still see a thin gleam between them. He pulled the seat belt out another few inches and looped it over her palm. Her fingers curled around it, but she didn't finish pulling it over herself to fasten.

Nor did he move his hand away.

"What am I thinking now?" The thought unconsciously emerged in a whisper that made her cheeks go hot.

He was silent for so long she thought he wouldn't answer. And even though it would be better and easier if he didn't, if he pretended he hadn't heard what she hadn't meant to say—aloud, anyway—she badly wanted to know.

"You're not thinking." When he finally spoke, his tone was even deeper than usual.

Her chin angled upward. She gave him a sideways look. "Is that so?"

His fingers slid from the seat belt and grazed her throat above the collar of her coat. They should have felt cold against her skin. It was cold outside. He wore no gloves.

Instead, his fingertips seemed to leave a trail of fire in their wake.

She held herself very still, afraid to even draw a breath when his fingers finally stopped, right beneath her chin.

His fingers nudged slightly, pushing upward. "You're feeling." Inches separated them and his conclusion whispered over her lips. "You wanted to know what bothered me yesterday if it wasn't Chloe?"

She made a faint sound of agreement. It was all she could manage.

"This." He closed the distance between them and covered her lips with his.

The kiss was brief. Searing. And when he lifted his head a moment later, she was quaking right down to the toes curling inside her boots.

"I'm feeling it, too," he said. His voice was still low. But a hardness had entered it. "And feeling is one thing I'm never going to do again."

He straightened, letting the cold air sweep between their bodies again in the moment before he slammed the door shut.

But the air was no colder than the shivers caused by his words.

Chapter Six

Ryan saw the tall, white-haired man the second he left J.D.'s barn.

He was standing near the back porch of the house, easily visible across the open distance and the various pickups and horse trailers parked there. Which probably meant he was coming down from the house and his cousin would have had no reason not to tell Coleman Black where Ryan could be found.

On top of the weekend he'd just had—not just learning about Chloe, but that monumentally unwise kiss he'd given Mallory the evening before—the sight of his onetime boss did nothing to improve his afternoon.

He left the barn door open behind him and started crossing toward the house and the man who was closing the distance even more rapidly.

Cole removed the thin cigar clenched between his teeth. "It doesn't make my day having to traipse out here," he greeted flatly. "I assume you got the background report you requested."

Ryan just nodded and walked past him. He dumped the tack, which he intended to take into town for some repair work, into the back of his truck.

"You haven't returned my calls," Cole continued. "Haven't answered my letters. My e-mails." The dossier Cole had provided had proved every word that Mallory had told him. It had also made Ryan feel cold inside that he'd even ordered it. But trust didn't come easily. Not after all these years.

"Most people would get a clue." Ryan eyed Cole's cigar, but it wasn't lit so he had no reason to tell him to get rid of it. Ryan didn't smoke around J.D.'s place—mostly because his cousin tended to get pretty pissy about a habit that was never a good idea around a barn, anyway. And he didn't see why Coleman should have the pleasure, if he didn't.

Too bad Ryan's fingers fairly itched right now to pull out a cigarette and light up. "Just because I called in a favor for the report doesn't mean anything more. There's nothing else to say and nothing I want to hear," he told Cole. "So instead of bugging me, why don't you go spoil someone else's day?"

Cole could call on Ryan's uncle, Tristan, who was still deeply involved in the agency despite his highly successful company, CeeVid. Or he could drive down to visit Ryan's cousin, Angeline, who was married to Brody Paine, though he figured Angel would be more welcoming than Brody. Brody might be Cole's son, but from what Ryan had heard, that surprising relationship was anything but easy.

"You can't walk away from our biggest case like you did and expect us to just forget about it."

"I turned over everything I knew," Ryan countered. He'd sent the few shreds of evidence he'd managed to collect during those three hellish years, along with his notes, through a secure channel before he'd deliberately and carefully dropped below the radar.

Knowing that the sum total of his work wasn't anywhere near enough to bring charges against the people involved in the trafficking ring, much less garner a conviction, was just one more weight of failure.

"Krager has resurfaced outside of Prague."

Ryan flinched. He didn't even want to hear the name of the elusive man who'd headed the ring. "Not my problem."

"You knew him better than anyone."

He glared at Coleman. "And look how far that got us. For every auction house that closes down, three more up in its place." Not to mention the casualties they'd racked up in the process. The lives that had been lost.

He walked around Cole, heading toward the fenced corrals situated near the barn. J.D. was still laid up with her shoulder and Ryan had promised her new fiancé, Jake, that he'd get the horses exercised before J.D. got it into her head that she felt good enough to do it herself.

Which, knowing J.D., was pretty likely.

"I want you to come back to the agency," Cole's voice followed him.

Ryan shook his head. He snatched the halter and lead off a fence post where he'd left it earlier and opened the corral gate enough to get inside. He gave a sharp whistle and three of the five horses he'd let out earlier came trotting over. "No."

"You belong there."

He gave Cole an incredulous look. "You must be desperate for agents."

"I don't want you just as an agent," Cole returned evenly. "I want to put you in charge of our international cases."

Ryan took his time sliding the halter over one of the horse's heads. He'd chosen Bonneville, one of J.D.'s more recalcitrant boarders, but the ornery buckskin was surprisingly docile for once. "No." He clipped the lead rope in place.

"It'd be a similar position to your uncle's," Cole continued, as if Ryan hadn't spoken. "Only instead of domestic cases they'd be international."

"Is that supposed to be tempting?" He pushed open the gate again, leading the horse out, then circling him around again so he could reach the gate to close it. "You handle international." And oversaw everything else.

"Maybe I'm thinking about retiring."

Ryan snorted. Coleman had been running the agency for so long he was synonymous with it. He'd die running the place. "Right." He tied off the horse and went back into the barn. Cole was still standing there waiting when he came out again with the blanket and saddle.

"I need people like you," Cole continued.

Ryan settled the blanket on Bonneville's back, staring blindly at the soft red-and-black check. "I walked out on a case," he said needlessly, since no one knew that better than his boss. More than that, though, Ryan had walked out on his life.

If he went back, he was pretty sure whatever was left of his humanity would die. And then he'd have no life at all.

Bonneville's head craned around, his teeth snapping.

"Cut it out," he snapped back, and the horse heaved out a breath, shifting. He shook his head, his black mane swishing. But the beast didn't attempt another nip and Ryan reached for the saddle, sliding it on Bonneville's back.

"Looks like a horse who doesn't want to be bugged."

Ryan smiled grimly, deftly working the straps and pulling down the stirrup that had been folded up. "Maybe Bonneville and I have more in common than I thought," he said pointedly. "Go back to Connecticut, Cole," he advised. He picked up the bridle and the metal bit jangled softly as he carefully directed it toward the horse. But Bonneville let him slip the bit between his teeth without complaint. "I'm done."

"Even though you can do something about Krager and people like him."

Ryan gathered the reins in his hand and swung up in the saddle. "Krager's untouchable." He'd had to face that unpalatable truth more than once. "He buys his protection from all the right people and he keeps his head down better than anyone I've ever seen."

"Scum like that are never untouchable."

"Then find someone who believes that and put *him* on the case." He clucked softly and Bonneville bolted past Cole.

With the cold air blasting over Ryan's face, he let the horse run as far and as fast as he wanted, and when they finally returned to J.D.'s place, a light snow had begun to fall.

And Cole was gone.

He unsaddled the horse, turned him into his stall in the barn and was brushing him down when J.D. came to find him. "You got a message," she told him.

He had no trouble imagining what Cole might have said in it.

"From Dr. Keegan."

He stopped brushing and looked over at his cousin. Confusion warred with curiosity in her green eyes. "What did she want?"

"Don't know. She just asked that you call her." J.D. handed over a scrap of paper. "There's the number."

He glanced at the number on the paper and slid it into his pocket, though he could have just as easily thrown it away. Once he saw a number, he never forgot it.

"So…" J.D. rubbed her chin with the knitted shawl she had wrapped around her shoulders. "I'm pretty sure you're not pregnant, so why is my O.B. calling you?"

He lifted his eyebrow. The rest of the family would know soon enough about Chloe, if they weren't already whispering about it behind his back. "Why do you think?"

She looked slightly amused. "Have anything to do with the two of you kissing in the hospital parking lot last night?"

He grimaced. Even in an empty parking lot, there was no privacy in this town. "Don't you have a fiancé to bug?"

Her faint smile widened and, evidently satisfied at the reaction she'd gotten out of him, she strolled from the barn.

The second she was out of sight, Ryan went into the tack room, yanked up the receiver on the old-fashioned rotary-style phone that hung on the wall there and dialed the number Mallory had left.

She answered on the second ring. "Ryan?"

"What's wrong?" Her voice sounded muffled. "Are you all right?"

She made a soft sound. "I'm not even going to wonder how you know something's wrong."

His grip tightened on the hard plastic receiver. "What is it?"

"I wasn't even sure if I should call you, but—"

"Mallory."

"Right." She sounded unaccountably rattled. "It's Chloe, actually. She had an accident on the playground. We're in the emergency room and—"

The world stopped.

"I'm on my way." He barely heard her start to speak again when he dropped the phone in its cradle.

Less than a minute later, he was in his truck aiming toward town and was soon pulling to a stop near the emergency room entrance.

Mallory was standing at the desk, her waving hair falling over her cheek as she focused on the papers she was completing. The silvery-gray suit she wore was perfectly tailored and only hinted at the curves beneath, and he had the out-of-place realization that he'd never seen her dressed so formally.

Obviously the sound of the automatic doors at his entrance alerted her and she looked over her shoulder.

He wasn't sure which was redder—her nose or her eyes—and the core inside him that had gone tight and stayed tight from the second he'd heard her voice on the phone went even tighter.

He crossed to her side, taking her shoulders, trying to read her face before she could deliver whatever awful news she had. "Is she alive?"

Alarm flashed through her eyes. Her forehead knitted. "God, Ryan. *Yes.* She only has a fracture. Not that a fracture is only an *only.*" She pressed her lips together as if to stop the words gurgling out of her.

His knees nearly went out from beneath him and only when he saw the wrinkles in the smooth fabric of her suit did he realize just how deeply his fingers were digging into her shoulders. He deliberately loosened his grip. "What the hell happened? What did Chloe break?"

She swallowed. "Her arm. The, um, the kids were outside for lunch recess and she fell off the—" she gestured with her hand and seemed to realize she was still holding the pen at the same time "—the bar things."

"Monkey bars," another voice provided beside them.

Ryan looked at the young nurse. She had long, honey-blond hair and brown eyes that were the same color as her mother's.

His mother's.

She was his baby sister. She'd been a laughingly scattered college student when he'd left Weaver. Now, she was a very beautiful, very composed young woman. "Courtney."

"Ryan." Her smile was painfully cool and he knew he'd earned it because, in the months he'd been back in Weaver, he'd gone out of his way to avoid her. Even more than being around his folks, his sister's company was an edge that was that much sharper.

It was young women just like his sister who'd been the most prized on the auction block. A block he should have been able to crumble. But he hadn't. And a girl who'd needed him just as much as Courtney ever had, had died as a result of that failure.

Courtney didn't look at him now as she picked up the clipboard holding the sheaf of papers that Mallory was in the process of completing. "You can finish these back there, Dr.

Keegan," she offered. "They'll be bringing Chloe back from radiology any minute."

"Thanks, Courtney." Mallory looked back at Ryan again. "Do…do you want to come with me?"

His sister's face was full of questions about what was going on between him and Mallory, but she didn't voice a single one. And if she knew about him kissing Mallory the way that J.D. had known—which she probably did, considering the effective grapevine—he was glad she didn't feel compelled to comment.

She simply thumped the button on the wall that automatically opened the double doors that closed off the waiting room from the action, and preceded them through. Her white shoes squeaked softly on the tile floor as she pushed through yet another door and disappeared from sight.

Mallory headed for the first bed that was only partially shielded by the curtain hanging from the ceiling track. She moved a puffy purple coat and an equally purple backpack from one of the molded-plastic chairs situated near the bed and set them on the floor, then gestured to the seat. "Might as well get comfortable if you're going to stay."

"If?"

"I wasn't sure what you'd want to do." She didn't look at him. Nor did she take the second empty chair, or the round, rolling metal stool, but remained standing next to the high counter alongside the bed. "After what happened last night, I mean."

"After I kissed you, you mean," he corrected bluntly.

Her pale cheeks flushed. "And after what you said."

He hadn't said a word on the short drive to her rented house after they'd left the hospital. But then, neither had she.

Instead, she'd bolted from the truck when his wheels had barely stopped turning in front of her house, and ran up the front walk as if she couldn't wait to get away from him.

"Yet you called me now, anyway."

Her lips parted softly, but it was a moment before any

words emerged. "You had a right to know." Then she set the clipboard on the counter that was complete with a small stainless sink and bent her attention over the forms again.

But as he watched, she didn't seem to do anything but click at the end of the ballpoint pen.

He ignored the chair and slid the pen out of her restless grip and tossed it onto the counter. Her eyes flew up to his.

"When did you get here?"

"Almost an hour ago." She grimaced. "She was already here, I'm afraid. The ambulance brought her from school when they didn't reach me directly."

"You were at your office?"

"I was with a patient." Her wan face tightened. "Nina didn't give me the message until after Mrs. Baker left."

"And Nina is…?"

"Nina VanSlyke. The office manager who makes every day spent with her a delight." She visibly gathered herself. "When I left there, she was in the process of canceling the rest of my appointments for the day. She wasn't particularly happy about it."

From what he could tell, Nina sounded like a bitch. "Finish telling me what happened. Chloe was playing on the monkey bars, and…?"

Mallory was wearing a thin, off-white blouse that peeked above the narrow V of her fastened jacket and he could see the fine shimmer of her pulse beating at the base of her throat against the unadorned neckline. He had a fleeting thought of a hummingbird in flight.

"She was hanging by her arms and doing some sort of flip to the ground." Her voice was shaking. "You know how kids do."

He didn't, but wasn't going to stop her.

"Anyway—" she brushed her hair behind her ear "—she landed badly and…and here we are." Her smile was weak and devoid of humor and her gaze suddenly shifted away, but not before he saw the glisten of fresh tears. She dashed her fingers over her cheeks. "Sorry," she mumbled. "I'm not very good with this sort of thing."

He peeled off his jacket and dumped it on the chair. "You handle medical emergencies pretty often."

"Not ones concerning the people I love." She snatched a tissue out of the box on top of the counter, blew her nose and then washed her hands.

She didn't pick up the pen again, or even look at the paperwork, but paced over to the door that Courtney had gone through and pushed it open. She looked up and down the corridor there and paced back again, the door swinging slowly shut behind her.

The more she paced, the more his own clawing need to do so seemed to lessen. "Why do they send the kids outside for recess when it's snowing?"

She'd folded her arms across her chest, but even from where he stood, he could see how white her knuckles were.

"I think they try not to keep them inside unless it's really inclement weather. What's a few snowflakes to a child?"

"Aren't there playground monitors or teachers or somebody to keep the kids from doing anything dangerous?"

"Yes." She was gnawing at her lower lip. "But the kids aren't supposed to be jumping off the playground equipment like that, anyway. Which Chloe was well aware of. They had the same rule at her school in New York. One of the rules that she broke pretty frequently, I'm afraid."

He was well aware of the accidents that could happen on a playground, and had broken more than a few school rules when he was a kid, too, though his infractions had generally been more along the line of smoking or ditching classes.

Something told him, however, that Mallory had been one of those students who'd always followed the straight and narrow.

"I thought she'd be done doing that sort of thing once we came here, though." She paced across the silent emergency room floor again. When she got to the end, she pulled up her cuff to look at the slender black watch on her wrist, then turned on her heel and paced back again. "I don't know what's taking them so long."

"It's definitely broken?"

"Definitely." She paled all over again. "It's closed—no broken skin—but…" She broke off, looking more than a little ill.

"She'll have a cast?"

"Probably. But hopefully they'll just be able to set it and she won't need surgery." She folded her arms again, looking as if she was barely managing not to fly apart. "I'm not good at this," she whispered again.

She was killing him.

He went over to her and pulled her into his arms. She resisted for a moment but, after a shuddering breath, almost seemed to collapse into him. The top of her head rested beneath his chin and he gathered her even closer.

He tried not to notice that amid the sterile, antiseptic hospital smell surrounding them, her hair smelled like fresh lilacs and that the silky soft suit she wore skimmed over curves that fit painfully well against him.

"Nobody likes hospitals," he said gruffly.

Mallory laughed brokenly. "Not like this," she agreed.

She still felt shaky and, against her, Ryan's chest felt wonderfully steady. His arms around her wonderfully strong. He smelled of hay and leather and a vague tinge of tobacco, and even though she knew she shouldn't let herself lean on him in any way—much less emotionally—she couldn't make herself move away.

Her eyes closed and she let out a breath.

She hadn't lied when she'd told him why she'd phoned him. But she hadn't told the entire truth, either.

That her immediate reaction had been to call for him even *before* she'd qualified his right—as Chloe's father—to know what had happened.

"Did you call your grandmother?"

Once again, Ryan seemed to be eerily attuned to her thought processes. She was afraid she was beginning to get used to it. "Yes. It's better that she not come to the hospital, though. She had a bad bout with the flu last year and has been susceptible to viruses since." It was the closest she'd gotten to losing her precious grandmother and it wasn't anything she wanted to repeat.

"No place better than a hospital to pick up a germ. Why'd you decide to be a doctor?"

"I was good in maths and sciences." His hand swept slowly down her spine, then back up again and she felt herself sinking even more into his chest. "My mother died of breast cancer when I was fifteen," she found herself admitting without forethought.

"That's right." His voice rumbled through his chest against her ear. "I remember Cassie mentioning that."

At the reminder of her sister, Mallory unearthed some willpower from some reserve she didn't even know she possessed, and straightened away from Ryan.

His arms immediately fell away.

He clearly had no problems letting go.

She brushed back her hair as well as the unwelcome observation.

"What was she like?"

The question was unexpected. "My mother? She was… hardworking." Overworked. "Independent." Lonely.

Mallory shut off the mental editing that had only come into play once she'd been old enough to recognize the other side of the coin that had been her mother's life. And recognize, too, the similarity to her own life. "She left Ireland against Gram's wishes when she was a college student. They didn't speak for years."

And only when Gretchen Keegan had two teenage daughters barely a year apart in age with no father for them around, and a diagnosis of cancer, had she broken that silence. Gram and her mother had only had a short while together after that.

"She had a beautiful smile and she sang when she cooked," she finished abruptly, and turned away from him. "I started out in med school with grandiose ideas of finding a cure for cancer, of course." Her attention fell on the clipboard with no small amount of relief, and she picked up the pen lying next to it. "But along the way I realized I was better suited for a different course."

"Delivering babies?"

"Yes." She focused on the forms and, striving for some semblance of neat penmanship, began filling in the lines. "I know it might sound clichéd, but there's nothing like helping to bring a new life into the world."

"Including Chloe."

Her hand suddenly shook, turning her letters into an illegible scratch. She nodded, unable to form a simple "yes" and rewrote her street address above the messy scribble.

"It can't have been easy."

She angled her chin, staring hard at the form and the signature line at the bottom of it for the responsible party.

She wished he would drop it.

Knew that he wouldn't.

"Letting my sister die? No." She scratched her signature over the line and set down the pen. "It wasn't easy."

Chapter Seven

Mallory barely had a chance to see the frown cross Ryan's face before the rattle of a wheelchair yanked her attention around to see Chloe being wheeled into the room.

Her daughter's arm was splinted and resting on a pillow in her lap. Her blue eyes were shadowed, her face unusually pale.

It took everything Mallory possessed to keep another rush of tears at bay. "Hey, baby." She crouched next to the wheelchair and smoothed back Chloe's bangs. "How're you doing?"

"I wanna go home."

"I know. Soon." She leaned forward and kissed her forehead, then rose to face the acne-skinned technician from radiology. "I'd like to see the films, Richie."

The young man swallowed, looking nervous. "Dr. Jackman will go over them with you, Dr. Keegan."

Mallory eyed him. "I'd like to look at them, first." She *was* a physician with privileges at the hospital, something he well knew.

"Sorry, ma'am. Policy." The kid quickly ducked out the door.

Swallowing her irritation, she ran her hand down Chloe's hair again. They'd given her some pain medication already, but had kept the dose as mild as possible. "Are you in pain?"

"Ever had a broken arm?" Ryan asked wryly.

He hunkered in front of the wheelchair, looking into Chloe's face. "Hurts like something nasty and eight-legged, doesn't it, sweet pea?"

A wisp of a smile touched Chloe's lips. "What're *you* doing here?"

He gently wriggled the toe of her green boot. "Wanted to see for myself how you were doing."

A knot formed in Mallory's throat at the pure delight that suddenly shone out of Chloe's face. "Really?"

"Really."

There was a mile-wide streak of gentleness in him that Mallory could recognize, even if he didn't want her to, and it made her feel weepy in an entirely different way.

"Hey there." Rebecca Clay stuck her head through the doorway and her warm gaze immediately fastened on the sight of her son and Chloe. "I heard what happened. How's the patient?"

Since Rebecca had directed the question at Mallory and not Ryan, she answered, telling his mother that they were still waiting for the radiology report. "Otherwise," she said, rubbing her hands over her crossed arms, "she seems pretty perky." Which was something attributable in no small way to Ryan's presence, she was certain.

"Speeding along radiology might be something I can help with," Rebecca said wryly.

She cast another glance at Chloe and Ryan, and Mallory felt a squeeze inside her at the longing that Rebecca was trying—and failing—to mask.

She strongly suspected that longing was rooted in more than just Rebecca's desire to get to know her granddaughter more fully. "Ryan's been great," she offered. "He's been waiting with me most of the afternoon."

Rebecca smiled. "It's good to have company," was all she said. "I'm due at a meeting, but I'll check on radiology for you first."

"Thank you." She wished she could divine the reasoning behind the palpable distance between Ryan and his mother. "I'll...I'll let you know what they find," she offered, and was glad that she had.

"I appreciate that." Rebecca looked touched as she quickly departed.

"That was generous of you," Ryan said without expression.

She wanted to ask him why *he* hadn't offered to keep his mother informed, but Chloe's presence had her refraining.

"Did you ever break your arm?" Chloe was asking him.

"Twice." For Chloe, he grinned. "I've also broken my leg and more 'n a couple of ribs."

Mallory strongly hoped her daughter didn't take after him in the broken-bones department.

"What about you?" She realized Ryan was asking her the question.

"Never broken a single bone," she said, and ironically felt she was on the outside of some elite group in which only he and Chloe were members.

More restless than ever, she headed toward the doorway, her high heels clicking on the tile, with the intention of finding John Jackman herself.

But the gray-haired man appeared before she reached the doorway. He held open the door, waiting for her to join him in the corridor, away from Chloe's hearing.

"Distal radius fracture," he said, cutting right to the chase. "Undisplaced. Pretty classic, given how she fell."

Relief made her feel dizzy. "No surgery, then." It might have been necessary if the fractured bone had been misaligned.

"Nope." He smiled slightly. "Splint until the end of the week and bring her back for another film to see her progress. We'll cast her then if the swelling is down enough. Courtney will be by in a few with the release orders." He patted her arm and turned to go, clearly a busy man, but he stopped and glanced back at her. "Heard about your work on Rhonda Danson, yesterday. Good job."

She smiled weakly. The last thing on her mind at the moment were patients. Maybe that made her a poor doctor.

Something that Nina would undoubtedly agree with.

"Thanks."

She returned to the emergency room and two sets of blue eyes turned toward her. She focused on the youngest, least disturbing pair. "The good news is we can leave soon. Bad news is you'll have to come back later this week to get a cast and in the meantime, *obviously,* no swinging from the monkey bars."

"I was just showing Jenny Tanner how Purple Princess flies from her castle tower to—"

Mallory lifted her hand. "I don't want to know. Were you following the rules on the playground?"

"Well, not 'xactly, but—"

"No, not exactly." This was another part of parenting that was no fun. "The rules are there for a reason, Chloe. To help prevent accidents just like this. Do you understand that?"

"Yes." Chloe's chin sank, glum.

Mallory could sympathize. She felt glum, herself. She always did whenever she had to chastise her daughter for something. But she'd do what it took if it meant protecting Chloe.

She still couldn't keep her stern expression in place, though, and leaned over her daughter, pressing their foreheads together. "I love you, okay? And I don't like seeing you get hurt."

"I'm sorry, Mommy," Chloe whispered.

"I know." She rubbed her nose over Chloe's and straightened.

Ryan was watching them, his jaw oddly tight, but the moment he realized she'd looked toward him, his expression relaxed.

Then Courtney reappeared to collect the paperwork that Mallory had completed and gave her another set to sign in exchange. "Not that you'll need them, but here are instructions on how to care for her arm this week, what to watch for, etc., and some tips for alleviating her pain." She handed over a stapled packet of papers. "I've written her return appointment on the top sheet."

"Thanks, Courtney." Mallory folded the papers in thirds and slid them into her pocket. Then she draped Chloe's coat around her daughter's shoulders.

The young nurse smiled and pulled a bright orange sucker out of her pocket. She handed it to Chloe and took hold of the wheelchair. "Ready to blow this pop stand, kiddo?"

She thought she heard Ryan make some sound, but when she looked, he was merely pulling on his leather jacket. His expression unreadable, he followed them through the double doors to the waiting room.

"I'll bring my car up to the curb," Mallory said, moving ahead of Chloe and Courtney.

She dashed out into the chill, which was considerably more noticeable now than it had been when she'd raced to the hospital several hours earlier.

"Where's your coat?" Ryan's voice followed her as she reached her car.

She dashed a snowflake off her cheek and yanked open her car door. "I forgot it at the office." Her keys were in the ignition, right where she'd left them, but when she turned them, nothing happened but a halfhearted groan from the engine.

She exhaled and dropped her head onto the steering wheel. "What else can go wrong with this day?"

"Sounds like the battery," he said.

"Probably." She didn't move.

"I have jumper cables in my truck."

She finally lifted her head. "You're going to get tired of rescuing me pretty soon."

He pulled off his coat and tossed it on her lap. "At least this kind of rescue I can pull off." He pushed the car door shut.

Which left her to wonder what kind of rescues he hadn't pulled off.

Her hands closed around the soft leather coat as she watched him jog back to his pickup, illegally parked near the emergency entrance.

A few seconds later, he was driving around near her car, positioning the front of his truck alongside the hood of her car. "Pop your hood," he said, through the window, while doing the same with his truck.

She fumbled around for the latch and evidently took too long, because he opened her door again, reaching inside himself, down near her knee. She barely heard the soft release of the car's hood, because she was altogether sidetracked by his closeness.

The only thing she seemed able to think about was that kiss, and the fact that his head was presently only inches from hers.

"Do about as much tinkering with cars as you do with plumbing?" His voice was low. Tinted with a dry humor that was all the more appealing for its rarity.

"Pretty much," she admitted faintly.

His focus dropped to her mouth and her heart seemed to stop.

In that moment, she felt acutely aware of everything around them. The low rumble of his truck engine still running; the whisper-soft feel of a snowflake that drifted through the open door to land on her hand and melt; the distant slam of a car door.

"I'll tell you when to turn it over."

He had the most amazingly shaped lips. "Turn what over?"

"The engine."

She blinked, yanked out of whatever mesmerizing spell he seemed to weave just by breathing. "Okay." She rolled her eyes in exaggeration, as if that would prevent either one of them from noticing her burning hot cheeks. "Duh."

His lips curved a little as he straightened, and she realized he had the faintest of dimples beside the corner of those spectacularly formed lips.

"Put the coat on," he advised, interrupting her wayward thoughts yet again before nudging the car door closed.

She decided that working the coat around her shoulders while still seated behind the wheel was ever so much more preferable to being caught ogling him some more.

It took him no time at all to lift the hood of her car and then he disappeared from view for a moment; poking his head around the edge of the uplifted hood to tell her she could try starting her car.

She turned the key and the engine immediately fired to life. He let the hood drop back into place, holding the thick jumper cables in one hand. "Keep the engine running until you get home," he said. "I'll follow you."

The offer was meant to be reassuring, she felt certain, but the only thing it accomplished was to send nervous anticipation zinging through her all over again.

He returned to his truck, which she realized had a smoother-sounding engine than her much newer car, and she drove around to the hospital doors. She stopped long enough to pick up Chloe from the wheelchair that Courtney had wheeled out of the hospital and, once she'd fastened her daughter's seat belt around her, drove out of the lot.

"Is Mr. Ryan your boyfriend?"

Mallory's hands tightened on the steering wheel and she shot Chloe a startled look. "No! Of course not. Why…why would you even ask that?"

"'Cause he's always around now, and Miss Courtney said

she thinks he must like you a lot, 'cause he's not around nobody that much. She told me he's her big brother, you know."

"I know." The reflection of his ancient truck behind her car seemed to consume her rearview mirror.

"If you and him had a baby, then I could be a big sister."

"Chloe!" She let out a shocked laugh. "Mr. Ryan and I are not thinking of doing any such thing."

"But I wanna be a big sister. And you wouldn't have to get married." Her daughter seemed to think that would make the scenario more attractive. "Even though you said that's where babies come from. I know, 'cause Lea Rasmussen in my class said her cousin was getting a baby and she wasn't married. And Grammy said my other mommy didn't ever get married, too. That's how come I don't got a daddy."

"Don't *have*." Her hands felt suddenly damp around the fleecy steering wheel cover, the leather of Ryan's coat that she wore almost suffocatingly warm. "And when were you and Grammy talking about all of this?"

Chloe leaned her head against the door as if her spurt of energy had dwindled. "I dunno. When I was little."

"Ah." Mallory didn't know whether to be amused or disturbed, and fell somewhere in between. She slowed to turn onto her street and glanced at the rearview mirror again.

Ryan was still there. Large as life.

Her hands strangled the steering wheel a little more. "Why didn't you ask *me* about your daddy?"

"'Cause you get sad."

"I do get sad that your other mommy isn't here. She was my big sister."

"Yeah." Chloe flopped her head onto her other shoulder, looking up at Mallory with her enormous blue eyes. "But you also get sad 'cause you don't got your own daddy."

Her jaw slid around a little as she absorbed that. "Grammy tell you that, too?"

Chloe shook her head. Her lashes drooped a little more. "Uh-uh. Can I sleep in your bed tonight?"

Tenderness plowed over her. "Sure."

"Can I have a puppy?"

She smiled slightly. Chloe's effort did as much to prove how resilient she was as anything could. "Nice try. What would we do with a puppy when we have to go back to New York?"

"We could stay here instead."

Mallory bit the inside of her cheek at that one. "What about your friends back home? Don't you miss them?"

"I like Jenny Tanner. She's my bestest friend, ever. And here we have a yard for a puppy." Chloe's voice was matter-of-fact.

"We talked about this before we came to Weaver," Mallory reminded her. "I'm only filling in for Dr. Yarnell until he gets back."

Staying in Weaver on a permanent basis had never been part of the plan.

Chloe just gave her a look as if to say that was a poor excuse in her opinion. Fortunately they'd arrived at the house, and Mallory turned into the narrow driveway that ran alongside the yard to the separate garage located just behind and to the side of the house. She drove past George the Great, who had begun sporting a scarf of shiny red Christmas garland in the past twenty-four hours and a red Santa hat that was now turning white with snow.

Instead of parking on the street as he usually did, Ryan turned into the driveway, too, and followed her all the way back. Before she could get out of the car to swing open the garage doors, though, he'd climbed out of his truck and was walking past her car, gesturing to stay where she was. He pulled open the heavy wooden doors of the old-fashioned garage with enviable ease, then stood to the side while she drove inside and parked.

She climbed out of the car and walked around to the passenger side, feeling awkward over his unexpected assistance. "Thanks."

She opened Chloe's door and carefully helped her out. "Can you walk okay?" She didn't want to chance Chloe slipping on the snowy ground, but she also didn't want to jostle her arm by trying to carry her.

"I'll get her." Ryan reached around her and easily scooped Chloe into his arms before she could protest.

Mallory had to swallow hard at the sight of him carrying her.

Since she'd brought Chloe home from the hospital as a newborn, carrying duty had been pretty much hers, and hers alone.

Now faced with the very real possibility that those days were going to change, she wasn't sure at all that she was prepared.

She tucked Chloe's coat more securely around her before he carried her out of the garage, then quickly retrieved her purse and briefcase from the backseat. Like the keys she'd left in the ignition, they, too, had remained forgotten in the car at the hospital while all of her focus had been on Chloe.

Her boots skidded on the frozen ground as she darted ahead of them up the back porch steps to open the door, but Kathleen must have seen their arrival. She was already waiting with the door open when they reached it.

"Aye, the poor girl," Kathleen tsked as they trooped through the door. She shut it after them and followed them into the kitchen, twisting her hands in the red-and-green apron tied around her waist. "What can I do?"

"She just needs to rest," Mallory assured. "And lunch was a long while ago for her."

"A long while ago for everyone, I imagine. It won't take me a minute to get some dinner on." Kathleen patted Chloe's uninjured arm gently. "I'll fix you up a tray and bring it to you."

"Thanks, Gram. The living room," Mallory told Ryan, and he carried Chloe through to the other room. She dumped her things on the kitchen table and avoided her grandmother's speculative expression as she followed.

Ryan was lowering Chloe onto one of the couches and Mallory grabbed a few pillows to tuck behind her back and another beneath her splint.

Chloe, it was plain to see, was staring up at Ryan as if he were even more wonderful than Purple Princess.

"I don't see how you can be comfortable on these couches," he said, straightening again.

Mallory smiled. "Don't knock 'em until you try them. I got them for a song at an estate auction, actually. And even though this place came with some furnishings, it was less expensive to move our stuff here than to pay storage for everything in New York until we go back."

"But if we stayed here," Chloe inserted quickly, "*then* could we have a puppy?"

Mallory eyed her daughter, shaking her head slowly. "Enough with the puppy."

"But—"

"What kind of puppy do you want?"

"Ryan—" Mallory turned her warning gaze onto the man. "Please don't encourage her."

"Relax, Doc." He sat down on the couch next to Chloe's feet. "We're just having a conversation, aren't we, sweet pea?"

Chloe's cheeks were still pale, but her sly grin was full of delight. "Yeah, Doc." Despite her giggle, she didn't tear her attention from Ryan's face. "And I want a *little* puppy that can sleep on my bed. One with white and brown spots and long, floppy ears."

"I had a dog when I was your age," he said. "Buster. He was a brown and yellow mutt that was so ugly he was cute."

"Did he sleep on your bed?"

"Yeah. But my mom didn't much like it," he said in a whispered aside.

"Conspirators," Mallory complained lightly, but there was a hitch in her throat and she went to the kitchen to see if she could help Kathleen.

It was hard to tell, though, whether the hitch was caused by the shine in Chloe's expression from Ryan's attention, or whether it was because she was suddenly facing the possibility that once Chloe knew that Ryan's interest in their family was entirely because of *her,* Mallory might well end up learning how it felt to be quite superfluous where Chloe was concerned.

Chapter Eight

Much to Chloe's delight, Ryan stayed through dinner.

And a short while later, when Mallory couldn't overlook the tiredness that her daughter had been valiantly trying to hide and proclaimed it to be bedtime, Chloe seemed to think it was perfectly natural to beg Ryan to carry her upstairs to bed.

Not that it seemed to take much begging, since Ryan seemed more than willing.

He scooped her off the couch and tipped her sideways so she could deposit a giggling kiss on her great-grandmother.

"I'll be up in a minute," Mallory said when they turned toward her. She'd need to help her daughter get ready for bed.

"I get to sleep in my mom's bed," Chloe told Ryan as they headed toward the staircase.

Mallory nearly choked when Ryan looked back in her direction over her daughter's head. "Makes you pretty lucky, I guess." His low voice was plainly audible.

"If I ever get a puppy, I think Buster would be a good name."

"And here I thought you'd want to name him or her Purple Princess," he teased as they went up the steps.

Kathleen caught Mallory's eye. "Smitten," she assessed, her low voice crisp.

"I hope you're talking about Chloe," she returned, just as crisply.

Her grandmother arched a white eyebrow and pushed herself out of her chair. "Maybe. Maybe not."

She reached for the tray that held the remnants of their meal, which they'd all eaten in the living room to keep Chloe company. Mallory waved her hand. "Don't worry about the dishes, Gram. I'll take care of them."

"I won't fight you for the privilege," her grandmother said easily. She moved past Mallory and patted her on the cheek in the same way she'd been doing since she'd come to the United States and met her teenage granddaughters. "There's a holiday program on the television I want to see, so I'm just going to turn in and watch it from bed."

Mallory wasn't fooled. Kathleen was making herself scarce. "Ryan is only here because of Chloe," she said softly, but was well aware that she was reminding herself just as much as her grandmother. "So I hope your thoughts aren't of the matchmaking variety."

"You're a beautiful woman who's not getting any younger," Kathleen reminded.

Mallory gave a wry laugh. She was thirty-three. "You're going to have me feeling like I'll have to show my teeth to my next suitor."

"*Next* suitor," Kathleen repeated, shaking her head. "There'd have to be a first for there to be a next."

"Another lovely reminder." Mallory sighed. "Regardless of the desert my love life has been since Brent and I broke up, thinking that anything might—" she sighed again "—with *him,* is out of the question. Gram, just yesterday you weren't even convinced that I'd done the right thing by bringing us all to Weaver in the first place."

"That was yesterday," Kathleen said blithely. Her head perked upward even before Mallory heard Ryan's footsteps on the stairs and she headed out of the living room. "I'm off to bed," Mallory heard her tell Ryan. "Thank you for what you've done today."

"Didn't do much." His voice was gruff.

"Ah. You were here now, weren't you?"

Mallory couldn't resist turning her head and looked over her shoulder in time to see her grandmother pat Ryan's hand as she passed him on her way to her bedroom. Like Mallory's office, her grandmother's room was located at the rear of the rambling old house.

And without her grandmother's presence, Mallory was acutely aware of Ryan's.

She pushed off the couch, restlessly brushing down her slacks, and headed toward the stairs.

Toward him.

"I should get up to Chloe," she offered somewhat obviously. "Thank you for carrying her up. She could have walked, or…or I could have carried her." But her daughter had wanted *him*.

He nodded, silent.

She needed to get Kathleen's comments—and Chloe's— about him out of her head. They were seriously messing with her equilibrium.

Or maybe that was simply caused by standing a foot away from him and breathing in the same air.

Her cheeks felt hot.

She put her hand on the newel post, her foot—bare since she'd kicked off her high-heeled boots and thin socks after eating—on the first riser. "I'll just go up, then." She wasn't certain if she was waiting for a response from him or not and she went up a few more steps.

"She's a good kid."

Her fingers tightened over the polished wood banister. "Yes."

He watched her for a moment longer, then nodded once and turned away from the staircase.

She hesitated, but he said nothing else. Certainly not a word of goodbye.

She wasn't relieved. Nor was she disappointed.

Not exactly.

Mostly, she couldn't quite identify the oddly incomplete sense she had, but taking her cue from him, she remained silent as well as she continued up the stairs.

Chloe was sitting at the head of Mallory's sleigh bed, propped up by a mountain of pillows and looking much like a pampered little princess, if not for the sling. "I'm going to get your nightgown," she told her as she passed the room.

"The purple one," Chloe called after her.

No surprise there.

Mallory retrieved a clean nightgown from the chest of drawers in Chloe's room and went back up the hall to her bedroom, deftly helping her daughter out of the sling and her clothes, into the nightgown and back into the sling. She helped her brush her teeth and wash her face, and tucked her back into bed.

"Will you brush my hair?"

The exhausting day showed not only in the splinted arm but in the dark smudges beneath Chloe's eyes. "Only for a little while." She retrieved the mother-of-pearl-backed brush from her dresser and sat down beside Chloe, slowly drawing the natural bristles through her daughter's hair.

The brush was old and the ritual was one that lived on from Mallory's childhood. The brush had been her mother's and every night before Mallory and Cassie had gone to sleep, their mother had brushed their long hair and told them stories of growing up in Ireland.

Now, as Mallory stroked through the shining brown hair and Chloe's sturdy little body relaxed against Mallory's, she could almost believe that both her mother and Cassie were there with them.

"Mr. Ryan told me a bedtime story," Chloe murmured sleepily after about the tenth stroke.

"Did he? About what?"

"A little girl who gets lost from her mom and dad, but gets rescued after she finds a magic rock."

She swallowed her surprise and smoothed Chloe's hair back and ran the brush through it again. "Think you can sleep?"

"Mmm-hmm." To prove it, Chloe buried her cheek in one of Mallory's bed pillows. "Does Mr. Ryan got a job?"

"He works at his cousin's place." She repeated only what she knew about him from Rebecca. "He…fixes things."

"Like he fixed our bathroom?"

"Yes." She slid off the bed and kissed Chloe's smooth cheek. "Now go to sleep. I love you, sweetheart."

"Mr. Ryan calls me sweet pea."

"Yes, I noticed."

"I don't like peas. They're *green*."

And Chloe usually wanted to avoid eating anything green. It made vegetables in general a challenge.

Mallory smiled. Despite her daughter's misconception, she hadn't seen any indication that Chloe minded being compared to a green pea. Not when it came from Mr. Ryan. "A sweet pea is a very pretty little flower." She tucked Chloe's hair behind her ear. "I think that might be what he's referring to."

"Oh. Okay."

"And I think the wild ones are purple," Mallory added.

Her daughter looked even more pleased as Mallory shut off the light and left the room. She didn't close the door; she wanted to be able to hear her downstairs if Chloe needed her.

Only after she left the room did she realize she was still holding her mother's brush, pressed against her chest.

She descended the stairs, rubbing her thumb over the stubby, soft bristles before lifting it to run it through her own hair. She reached the bottom and released a long sigh.

"Is she asleep?"

She started.

Ryan was standing in the living room next to the gigantic Christmas tree that, as yet, was decorated only with numerous skeins of popcorn garland. Chloe had been adamant that they not add any more decorations until she could participate.

"She will be within minutes, I'm sure." Her thumb pressed against the brush bristles. "I thought you'd left."

His fingers were pushed into the front pockets of his faded blue jeans and his shoulders seemed to strain the seams of the faded black T-shirt he wore. "I almost did."

Feeling cautious, she balanced the hairbrush on the newel post and padded across the wood floor. With the distance of the couch length between them, she stopped at one end. "What…why'd you change your mind?"

He didn't immediately answer.

He pulled his hands from his pockets, looked up at the unadorned top of the tree and paced to the other side of the fireplace. "How did you find me?"

The question wasn't unreasonable. Nor was it unexpected. She just hadn't expected it right then.

Her gaze dropped to the tray of dishes that still sat on the coffee table between the couches. "It wasn't easy," she admitted, and caught a wisp of something ironic in his expression.

"Yet you didn't give up."

She hesitated. "Actually, I did. For a while." She moved around the couch to pick up the laden tray and carry it into the kitchen.

Farther away from the staircase.

At the far end of the hall, she could see the closed door of her grandmother's bedroom.

She looked at him. "Some coffee?"

He followed her. "I have the feeling I might be needing some of your grandmother's *kick* in it."

She smiled faintly, though there was really nothing humorous about the situation.

She set the tray on the counter next to the sink and began filling the coffeemaker. The normal, practical motions helped to soothe the edge off her nervous energy. "I told you already that Cassie didn't talk much about you. The only thing I had to go on was that she'd worked with you." She filled the water reservoir and couldn't help glancing at him.

His arms were folded over his chest and he was leaning his shoulder against the kitchen door—an easy escape?—but his expression was unreadable.

She focused on the coffee again. "Cassie never talked much about her job at HW Industries. She had an apartment in Connecticut."

"Hartford," Ryan added.

"Yes." She pushed the power button on the maker and it immediately began hissing and gurgling. "Gram and I were still in Queens."

"The same apartment building with a super?"

"Yes. We lived there with our mother. Then Gram came, and we're still there." Or were, since she'd sublet the place while they were in Wyoming.

She turned to face him, glad for the steadying force of the counter and cabinets behind her. "To be honest, at the time, I didn't think all that much about Cassie's reticence. I was pulling double shifts at the hospital and she was doing something with her linguistic degree that was earning her enough to afford a really nice place in Hartford. She visited occasionally; usually called to talk about the crazy neighbors living next door to her, or whatever movie she'd seen, what guy she was dating."

The comment earned no reaction, though she wanted to believe she hadn't been looking for one.

"Anyway, one weekend Cassie came to visit and announced that she'd quit her job." Mallory lifted her shoulders. "And that she was four months' pregnant." The coffeemaker hissed behind her. "Gram, of course, demanded more details, but Cassie wasn't cooperative and, for a while, we assumed that things had ended badly between her and the guy. Shortly before she—" she swallowed "—delivered, she wanted us to know that wasn't the case. That the father—Ryan—was a good guy. Someone she'd worked with. Someone whose life didn't need to be turned upside down by an unexpected baby."

He straightened and paced across the room. "Okay. So why'd she die?"

Mallory frowned.

The task of finding Ryan was one thing. Telling him about the rest, another.

"What does it matter? She's gone."

His gaze slid toward hers. "It matters because of what you said this afternoon."

"I was…emotional."

His eyebrows lifted slightly.

"I told you I'm not good with my own crises," she defended. "People say all sorts of things in stressful situations."

"Yeah. Usually what they most dearly believe. Or feel."

"And what do you say when *you're* under stress," she returned, her tongue miles ahead of her discretion.

"We're not talking about me."

She lifted her hands. "Everything lately seems to *involve* you."

"You're the one who came here to Weaver."

As if she needed any reminder that she'd brought all of this on their heads. "Yes. Another action I'm completely responsible for."

"You're not responsible for your sister's death."

Her throat ached. "You don't know anything about it."

"Then tell me why she died."

Her hands curled at her sides. The calmer his voice became, the more agitated she felt. "Because I wasn't a good enough doctor," she said abruptly, and hated the out-of-control way she felt. "And she was stubborn."

"I don't want an editorial. I want the facts."

"Those are the facts!"

"Mallory."

Her shaking fingers pulled at the single button on the front of her suit jacket that she'd kept on for the simple reason that her blouse beneath was practically transparent. And she hadn't wanted him to see that every time she looked at him, her nipples went tight. "It has nothing to do with why we're here."

"It has to do with you."

She exhaled. It was his tone that tore at her the most. She seemed no more capable of resisting anything to do with him than Chloe.

And there was danger in that.

"Cassie wasn't quite twenty-four weeks along when she was diagnosed with preeclampsia," she said abruptly. Once he knew the truth, he'd stop looking at her with that intensity that threatened to warm her through to her soul.

Her soul was just fine.

Perfectly warm. Perfectly independent.

She just needed…no, she *wanted* Chloe to have what she and Cassie hadn't had as children.

"What's that?"

She blinked, almost saying *a father,* but realizing with something akin to hysteria that she was supposed to be thinking about Cassie's death.

She realized she'd tugged the loose button right off her jacket when it came free in her hand.

She shoved it into her pocket, mentally reeling in her unraveling senses with the doggedness that had gotten her through med school.

"It's a condition marked by high blood pressure and a high level of protein in the urine." She knew she sounded remote but couldn't seem to help it. "Cassie developed it particularly early. The only cure for it is delivering the baby, but—"

"At twenty-some weeks, she wasn't far enough along for that," he concluded.

"Exactly." The coffeemaker gasped. "There are some remarkable cases of survival after such extreme prematurity, but the odds against it are enormous."

He made a soft sound that she couldn't interpret and she took down two mugs from the cupboard, finding it easier to continue if she wasn't facing those otherworldly blue eyes. "Cassie refused to consider any option but proceeding with the pregnancy."

Despite the risks. Despite the odds. Cassie had bet on carrying the baby.

Bet and lost.

"She went on bed rest, and we treated her as best we could to gain as many weeks for the fetus as possible. We knew she'd have to deliver early, but at that point, every day—every week—makes a difference to the baby. And Cassie was determined to give her child the best start at life as possible." She yanked the coffee carafe out much too early and a stream of coffee sizzled against the hot plate.

Ryan lifted the coffeepot out of her hand and set it on the counter. He turned off the steaming coffeemaker, looking into her face. "What went wrong?"

Everything.

She turned away from him again. Went to the refrigerator.

Maybe he took milk in his coffee. She yanked open the fridge door only to stare blindly at the shelves.

"Mallory—"

She shut the door again without retrieving a single thing from inside. "Her placenta separated from the uterine wall three weeks before we'd planned to induce. I was on duty that night—" She broke off. She hadn't even known at first that it was her sister on the table bleeding to death while the attending physician performed a C-section.

He muttered a soft oath.

"We couldn't stop the hemorrhaging. Cassie went into shock." She stared at her hands, but was only seeing the horror of that night in her mind. "She died."

"You didn't *let* her die."

Her hands curled into fists. "I couldn't talk her into terminating her pregnancy when she could have. I couldn't talk her into scheduling an earlier delivery. There were so many steps along the way that could have changed the outcome."

His hands closed over her shoulders, forcing her to face him. "They weren't your steps to take."

She didn't realize there were tears on her cheeks until he wiped his thumbs over them. "But—"

His thumbs moved down to cover her lips. "Don't do that to yourself. Cassie wasn't stupid. You've said yourself how determined she was where Chloe was concerned."

She wrapped her fingers around his wrists. They were like iron and too wide for her fingers to fully circle. "I should have worked harder to save Cassie that night."

Somehow, she found her wrists captured in his hands, instead, with no real idea of how he'd done it. "What *were* you doing?"

"Trying to get Chloe to breathe. But Cassie—" She broke off.

"Were you the only one in the room with them?" His grip was almost punishing in its intensity.

She frowned. "No. No, of course not." The O.R. had been

a freaking madhouse. It had been months before she'd been able to force herself back into one. She would have lost her residency if not for the leniency she was allowed in consideration of the situation. "But—"

"But nothing. Stop taking on the responsibility for her death as if it's yours alone to take! You did what you had to do under the circumstances. What more do you expect, Mallory?"

She looked up into his face. "Did you love her?"

Chapter Nine

Did you love her?

Mallory's question seemed to echo around the silent kitchen, but instead of fading into indistinctness, it seemed to only increase in volume until the words were reverberating very distinctly inside her head.

His eyebrows had pulled together over his sharp blade of a nose. He let go of her wrists. "What?"

For a very brief moment, she caught a glimpse behind the deep blue barrier of his eyes to the man inside, and what she saw there had only one description.

Grief.

She wished she could erase the words.

Or turn back time. If not turning it back to that awful night seven years ago, then turning it back to just a moment ago so she wouldn't have blurted out such a revealing question.

It was no wonder he didn't want to get involved with her.

Maybe he still loved Cassie. Maybe he avoided all entanglements because of that.

But if he'd loved Cassie, why had he let her slip out of his life? Mallory had believed her sister when she'd said she hadn't been in love with Chloe's father, but maybe Cassie had lied. Downplayed her feelings.

Confusion had never been Mallory's best friend, and it wasn't now.

It didn't help that she wanted to rub her hands over the tingling in her wrists where Ryan had held them, either. "It…it doesn't matter. It's none of my business."

"You tracked me down—somehow—and *that's* what you think is none of your business?" He finally moved across the kitchen again, only to pace back and stand in front of her before she could manage to draw in the long breath her equilibrium needed. "Speaking of which, you still haven't explained how you found me."

No, because she'd gotten caught up in baring the horrible details of why the real mother of his child wasn't the one standing before him now.

"It's late," she said, instead. "Maybe we should wait until another time." Wait until she'd had a chance to process the stark emotion she'd seen in him.

You mean, adjust to the fact that he must have loved Cassie, even if she hadn't loved him.

"It's not that late."

She begged to differ. Two days ago the man had walked into her house and everything had changed.

There wasn't one thing about Weaver that didn't have her in over her head. And that most particularly applied to Ryan Clay.

"I need to check on Chloe."

For a moment, it looked as if he wanted to argue. But he just lifted his fingers slightly as if to say, *Go.*

She escaped.

There was simply no other word for it.

She went upstairs and checked on Chloe who was sound asleep just like Mallory—if she'd been truthful—had expected her to be.

She straightened the edge of the blanket and crept out of the room. But how long could she hide out on the landing before Ryan would get suspicious?

Not long, since he'd left the kitchen and was looking straight up at her.

The knot in her chest was beginning to feel far too familiar. Ignoring it, as well as the stinging need to close herself in her bedroom and away from his prying eyes, she forced herself to go back down the stairs and return to the kitchen.

He'd filled the two mugs with coffee and they were sitting on the little round table by the window, but she didn't sit down on one of the chairs.

Nor did he.

Neither one of them really wanted coffee.

She closed her hands over the back of the wood-slatted chair. "After Cassie died, we were inundated with condolence cards from all over the world," she offered baldly. "Gram read through them at the time." Much the same, she supposed sadly, as she'd had to do when her daughter had died. "She saved them all for me, but it was over a year before I could face looking at them. When I finally did, though, one of the cards was from a man named Coleman Black."

Ryan's gaze sharpened, but he said nothing, so she forged on.

At least telling him this part didn't feel as though she was peeling back her skin. And it gave her something to focus on, other than what she'd seen in his eyes.

Or so she told herself.

"Mr. Black's note was…brief. I still have it if you want to see it." She didn't know why she'd offered that. What would he care that something had made her keep the note, tuck it inside her jewelry box where it remained to this day?

"We'll see."

She hesitated, but he'd gone silent again, leaving her with the sense that she'd stepped into something else sticky and uncomfortable.

She moistened her lips again. "Anyway, he expressed his regret and said that Cassie had been a wonderful employee and it was clear he'd been her boss. The envelope was with the card. It had a handwritten return address for HW Industries in Connecticut."

"You followed up on the address?" For some reason, he seemed surprised at that.

"It was only logical. But it still took me months before deciding to do that," she admitted. Chloe had been a toddler by then. Both Mallory and Gram had been exhausted trying to keep up with her; Mallory because of the continuing demands of her career and studies and Gram simply because of her age.

"So what prompted you?"

Her lips parted. "I had our pictures taken for Christmas." She hadn't even really remembered that until now. "Chloe's and mine. One of those inexpensive packages that the discount stores are always pushing around the holidays? I wanted Gram to have a nice picture of us." She had an identical framed eight-by-ten on her dresser. Her and little Chloe wearing matching red sweaters.

The little family. Only both of Chloe's real parents were missing.

"When I went to the address, I'd hoped to find this Black person if he was even still there, and see if he could provide any information about *you.*" She grimaced. "Obviously I shouldn't have let so much time pass, because the only thing I found there was a toilet paper warehouse, and even though

I asked around, nobody recalled him or Cassie *or* a company called HW Industries."

Ryan almost snorted.

He'd bet that was the stonewalling Mallory would have received.

People did not walk in off the streets and expect a sit-down with the elusive boss of Hollins-Winword. Which was in fact the real agency hiding behind the odd—and at times ironically appropriate—toilet paper manufacturer. Only Mallory had no way of knowing that. "And then what?"

"I went back to New York," she said. "I sent a letter to the address, explaining who I was and the information I was trying to find and hoped it would get forwarded to the company's new location. I assumed that it had because I didn't receive it back in the mail. I didn't get an answer, though, so I sent another. And another." Her amber eyes were lost in the past. "It was about a year after I'd given up thinking I'd get a response when I got one. Of sorts. It wasn't the letter that I'd expected or hoped for at all. It was a small box containing a few items that had belonged to Cassie. The note accompanying them said she'd left them behind when she'd left the company. An adventure novel, and a small cosmetics case." She looked up to the ceiling. "I was so discouraged I nearly tossed them out. But there was a postcard inside the book postmarked from here, in Weaver."

He remembered the postcard even before she finished recalling the details.

He'd mailed the card to Cassie from Weaver years ago. Back when he hadn't had a hole inside him where his soul used to be. "I told her if she ever got to this side of the country, to check out Weaver," he said.

Mallory's lashes drooped, hiding her expressive eyes. "The postmark was clear enough. And Weaver is small. There were only a few men named Ryan that I found listed anywhere in the area. One was an elderly man whom I ruled out. The other was some hotshot naval guy. The navy part didn't sound right, but he was at least about the right age."

He grimaced. He had been in the navy. He'd followed in his father's footsteps there. And if he'd have stuck to the navy, lives—more than just his own—might have been very different.

Instead, he'd had the astronomical ego to think he could accomplish more good by throwing in league with Coleman Black.

"Gram and I weren't entirely in agreement about contacting Chloe's father," she said after a moment. "Or I should say contacting the man I *suspected* might be her father."

"But you went ahead and did it. Why?"

"I told you. Chloe deserves to know she has a father."

"Even if the father isn't the kind of person you want him to be?"

She was worrying at her lower lip, drawing his attention in a way that wasn't wise.

At his question, though, a troubled frown replaced the nibbling. "But I knew that you were a good man. Cassie said so."

He'd known Cassie before he'd gotten involved with trying to bring down Krager. Cassie didn't know the man he was now. If she did, she'd have made damn sure he was nowhere near her…*their*…daughter.

"Anyway, when I finally tried to contact you—" Mallory's soft voice drew him back again "—I ended up reaching your parents. I didn't know what to say, so I just claimed to be an old friend of yours and that I was trying to catch up to you." Her lashes finally lifted. "Your mother was very kind on the phone, but she told me that her son—that *you*—were deceased. Something to do with the military, which again just made me wonder if I had the right man at all."

Ryan ignored the confusion she couldn't hide, but it was harder than it should have been. "Is that why you didn't tell her about Chloe, anyway?"

Her hands lifted, asking for understanding or expressing defense. He couldn't tell.

"Partly. I guess I realized that you could have gone into the service after you'd worked with Cassie. But I only had speculation to go on where you and she were concerned in the first place," she said. "Telling your mother that Chloe might be her grandchild when there were so many unresolved questions just didn't seem right. What if I'd been wrong? What if it ended up being just one more loss to her? Maybe that sounds like a poor excuse now, I don't know. I just believed that Chloe would grow up the same way that Cassie and I had."

"How's that?"

"Without ever really knowing anything about who we were or where we came from."

"You know who you are, Doc," he countered. "The guy who left your mother to raise two daughters is pretty immaterial. Look at everything you've accomplished."

A tide of pink rose in her cheeks and, even though he'd done his share of pushing her off keel, he was the one ending up feeling discomfited now.

"Anyway," she said, seeming anxious to deflect that sort of observation, "I never expected to meet your mother in person, but she attended a medical symposium in New York in September. I was participating on a panel there and afterward, she introduced herself to me. I remembered her name but I was very surprised that she remembered mine and that phone call I'd made a few years ago."

"What was the panel for?"

"I—" She shook her head slightly and raked her fingers through her hair, tucking it behind one ear. It slid loose again. "Uh…it was on pregnancy after thirty-five. Why does it matter?"

"Curious." As much as he wanted to know how she'd ended up finding him, he still found himself just as interested in sidetracking her. Nudging her off the well-defined course she seemed to follow.

Didn't make it right, but there it was.

She gave him another look that plainly told him she was trying to figure him out and failing. "What was much more stunning than her remembering me was her telling me that you were alive, after all.

"Your mom…she glowed when she told me. I didn't know what to say. But it doesn't matter because Gram arrived with Chloe in hand—they were meeting me in the city to see a matinee after the last lecture—and your mother took one look at Chloe and knew the truth. It didn't matter that there were *so* many things that made no sense about it. Your mother pulled out a wallet-size baby photograph of you from her purse to show me."

Mallory looked up at him. "It was astonishing. I could have been looking at a baby picture of Chloe."

He sat down on one of the hard chairs, trying to equate the mother he knew with the woman who hadn't breathed a word about any of this to him. "*She* talked you into coming to Weaver."

"She…encouraged it," Mallory allowed. "Dan Yarnell had been wanting to go on sabbatical but had no replacement for his practice and she suggested that I might be suitable."

"What else did she tell you?"

She hesitated. "She said that, well, that she believed you needed to know about Chloe just as much as Chloe needed to know about you. Particularly now."

"And why's that?"

Her lips pressed together. "We didn't get into particulars, exactly, Ryan. She had one miracle already—you weren't dead!"

He spread his hands, staring at his palms. "Why didn't you lay all this on me when you got to town? Why wait all these weeks?"

She didn't answer immediately. "I could tell you that I was focusing on getting settled at Dan's practice and making sure that Chloe was doing okay in her new school. Because no matter what happened with you, I was committed to staying here until Dan returns in March. And all that would be true…but mostly…" Her eyes looked apologetic. "Mostly, I was afraid."

He eyed her. There was good reason for her to be afraid, but there was no way in hell that she could even know *what* those reasons were.

Nobody knew.

Not his father. Not his cousin Axel who was about the closest thing that Ryan had once called a best friend. And certainly not his mother who—well intentioned or not—had a surprisingly manipulative streak hiding inside her that he never would have expected.

"Afraid of what?"

She made a soft sound. Seemed to hunt for words. "First, do no harm."

A tenet of every doctor. "This isn't a medical situation," he countered.

"But the premise still applies." She pulled out the chair opposite him and sat down.

The neatly groomed, unvarnished tips of her slender fingers brushed against him, leaving him feeling nearly scorched.

The urge to escape started to expand inside him like some deadly balloon. The only thing that kept his butt planted was the soft earnestness in Mallory's eyes.

It was the kind of earnestness that only people who'd never experienced real tragedy could exhibit.

Yet that didn't apply to Mallory at all.

Which made her a contradiction.

A very beautiful, very tempting contradiction.

One who was thankfully oblivious to the direction of his

thoughts, judging by her expression, which was as open now as it had been closed and almost frantic earlier.

"I respect your mother, Ryan. She's a brilliant physician and obviously devoted to her family. And…I like her. I like every member of your family whom I've met since I've come to town."

"Sometimes it feels like the only people in this town are family," he said gruffly. It was as much a curse as it was a blessing. And it was probably one of the reasons most of his cousins at one time or another felt some compulsion to leave.

Invariably, they came back.

Just as he had.

"Well, there are more people related to you than I even realized." Her soft lips curved upward. "Chloe's teacher, for instance." Her expression went serious again and he found himself wanting to get back that hint of amusement.

Amusement was so much easier than earnestness.

"So do I come here and immediately insert ourselves into your family's lives because I believe Chloe has a right to know who her father is without any thought to how it might affect any of them?" She looked away. "Even more importantly, how it will affect you?"

"You are a parent. You put the protection of your kid first," he said evenly. He realized his hands were curling into fists and he deliberately relaxed them again. Not all of the kids that Krager had bought and sold like a commodity had come from uncaring parents.

"And I do put Chloe's welfare first," Mallory retorted with some spirit. "I'm not naive, Ryan. There are people out there who have no business having children, much less raising them. People who are technically families who are worse than enemies could ever be. But that's *not* the Clays. Do you think I would have left a very busy career, pulled Chloe out of her school and yanked both her and Kathleen away from their friends if I hadn't done enough research about your family to know they weren't serial killers? Give me some credit!"

He shoved to his feet.

She was right.

The Clays, to a one, were all decent people.

Strong-willed and loving women.

Courageous and honorable men.

All of them heroic in some way, on a kaleidoscope of scales.

He was the one who hadn't lived up to the family legacy.

He was the one who had failed.

He was a Clay, but he didn't deserve the heritage or the name. Maybe once he had. But not anymore.

He wasn't the son his parents had raised. He couldn't be the son they wanted.

But they had a grandchild now. And that—that was one thing he could give them.

Because a young woman had once wanted a baby despite the danger. Because another young woman hadn't given up when she so easily could have. And probably should have.

What was it about the Keegan women?

He rubbed at the pain in his forehead.

He knew what it was about this particular Keegan and it had his guts tied into a knot.

"What'd my parents do when you arrived in town?"

Her hands spread, palms upward. "Do? Well, nothing. I mean your mother had already done a lot what with setting things up for me with Dr. Yarnell."

"They didn't come over to see Chloe? Didn't invite you to their place?" Like the rest of the family, his folks were big on...family.

She shook her head. "I think...your mother probably felt she'd done as much as she should without your knowing."

More likely, his mother had been afraid he'd cut and run.

Disappear.

And hadn't he been contemplating doing just that? Not just when Chloe had been at the diner with her do-gooder dollar but long before then.

And since then.

"Well, I know now," he said evenly.

"Right." She rose, brushing her palms nervously against her thighs. "So, what…how do you want to proceed?"

The lapels of her jacket parted, giving him a glimpse of curve-molding lace beneath that thin ivory blouse. And beneath that lace, the not so pale shadow of a very tight nipple.

He grabbed his coat from the back of the kitchen chair where she must have left it when they'd gotten back from the hospital with Chloe.

Yeah, he was escaping. But it was either leave now, or pull Mallory into his arms and delve beneath that jacket, that blouse and that lace. And once he started, he wasn't sure he'd be able to stop.

And that was something he'd never been afraid of before. He'd never known a woman who could make him question his own control.

She was watching him with a faint frown that tugged her level eyebrows closer over her patrician nose. "Ryan?"

"I'll arrange a meal or something with my folks," he said abruptly. "Tell 'em to mind their p's and q's since Chloe doesn't know anything, yet." His jaw tightened. "But at least they'll have a chance to start getting to know her."

Mallory's lips parted. She pressed her curled hand to the center of her chest. It only succeeded in drawing the thin fabric of her blouse more tightly against her breasts. "Okay." It was more of a breath than a word.

He pushed open the kitchen door.

The snowfall had gotten worse. No longer a few flurries, it was falling hard and fast.

Pretty much the way he felt around Mallory.

He looked back at her.

She was still staring after him. Hadn't moved an inch.

"I wasn't in love with Cassie," he said, then wished to hell that he hadn't when Mallory's amber eyes widened and she took a step toward him.

Involuntarily, he figured, judging by the way she pulled herself up short.

"Oh." A swallow worked down her lovely throat. "Okay."

Only nothing really was okay, and they both knew it.

So he stepped out into the blowing snow and pushed the door closed after him.

Chapter Ten

Mallory's hand hovered over the telephone situated on the corner of Dan Yarnell's oversize wood desk.

Should she call Ryan?

It was Wednesday afternoon. She hadn't heard from him since Monday night.

Not that he'd said how quickly he'd arrange something with his parents and Chloe, but for some reason she'd expected to hear from him by now.

Some reason?

That was a laugh. She didn't even have to close her eyes to summon up the memory of his face as he'd left her house the other night. The blue flame that had seemed to burn in his eyes when he'd looked at her.

A flame that had been a world away from any glimpse of grief.

I wasn't in love with Cassie. His deep voice whispered through her thoughts.

Her fingers curled into her palm. She drew her hand away from the phone without touching it. Annoyed with herself, she added the lab results she'd been studying to the medical file she'd been making notes on, slapped the folder closed and took it with her out to the reception area. "Dee Crowder was the last patient for the day, right?" Mallory set the patient file for the pretty elementary school teacher on top of Nina's rigidly organized desk.

Nina barely glanced up from her computer. "Do you have another appointment on your schedule?"

"Ah…no." She forced a smile. With the possible exception of having to reschedule her appointments the day that Chloe had broken her arm, Mallory couldn't think of any reason since she'd come to fill in for Dan that could have so thoroughly earned the woman's dislike.

"Why don't you cut out early," she offered, since it was only the middle of the afternoon. A few extra hours were usually welcomed, particularly at this time of the year when everyone seemed frantic to find more time for the holidays.

But the gray eyes that Nina turned on her looked glacial. "Dr. Yarnell's office is open until four o'clock every weekday."

"Well." Didn't she feel told off? "If you change your mind, feel free to take off." She let the matter drop and headed back to the office at the rear of the building.

Yarnell's setup was pretty straightforward. Four examining rooms, two on each side of the hallway leading back to his office. And in front of it all, was Nina the guard-dragon.

Feeling uncharitable and not liking it, Mallory closed the door to the office and sat down again behind the wide desk that she still didn't feel at home behind, despite the weeks she'd been there.

Ignoring the silent telephone, she picked up one of the framed photographs of Chloe that she'd positioned on the crowded credenza behind the desk and reminded herself that everything she'd done lately had been for her.

If it weren't for Chloe, she'd still be back in New York, where she was just one of a half-dozen low men on the totem pole in a practice that boasted eight partners. She'd have a never-ending back-to-back stream of patients to fit into too little time, and she certainly wouldn't end up with hours to spare.

She glanced out the window beside the desk. There was a house across the street, smack dab between an automotive garage and an antique store that had sported a large Closed sign from the day that Mallory had arrived. In the yard of the house, though, someone had built a snowman.

It was not as large as the one Chloe and Ryan had built before it had snowed, but it still made her smile a little.

It was short-lived, though, when her thoughts turned again, too easily, to the puzzle that was Ryan Clay.

She replaced the picture frame on the credenza next to the small aquarium that Nina had warned her not to disturb and pressed her hands over her face.

Why hadn't he called? Had he changed his mind?

Maybe the leisurely patient schedule wasn't such a good thing after all. It gave her too much time for wayward thoughts.

She let out a breath and pushed away from the desk again. Coat and purse in hand, she walked back out to Nina's desk. "I'm leaving," she said, stating the obvious.

Predictably, Nina looked disapproving. "You're the doctor."

"That's what all of those diplomas and certificates on the wall in the office say," Mallory returned. "Page me if you need me," she said, and walked out without waiting for the woman to explode.

Fortunately, Mallory wasn't working for Nina. Her agreement was with Nina's boss, Dr. Yarnell, and *he* was tramping around Asia somewhere for months yet.

Outside, she quickly pulled on her coat and climbed in her car. Thanks to the new battery that Ryan had put in, it started right up. Since she'd already done a round at the hospital, she didn't turn in that direction when she left the office, but headed, instead toward the shops that were located on Main Street.

A lot of the nurses at the hospital had recommended a particular shop there, Classic Charms, as a good place to find unusual gifts and Kathleen was still on her Christmas list to be taken care of. She'd make that her first stop. And after that, she'd hit Shop-World and make sure she was all set for Chloe's birthday party.

It was there, standing in line at the big discount store with a basket on her arm filled with little-girl trinkets to fill Chloe's gift bags with that she felt a tap on her shoulder and looked back to see the man-of-her-thoughts standing behind her.

He had a fifty-pound bag of dog food slung over his shoulder as if it weighed nothing.

"What are you doing here?" She realized she was probably staring at him like some infatuated schoolgirl.

He tapped the immense bag with an ironic finger. "Cheapest place to get it."

"I didn't know you had a dog." He hadn't mentioned it when Chloe was on her puppy tangent.

"Don't." He didn't elaborate. "I tried calling you about an hour ago. Your nurse said you walked out."

She exhaled. "She actually used that term?" She could tell by his expression that Nina had. "And she'd probably delight in using it with any patient who called in, too," she murmured. The customer in front of her was finished and she moved forward, setting her items on the conveyor belt. "The schedule was free and I told her to page me if she needed me."

"You don't have to justify yourself to me. You're the doctor."

She found herself smiling a little at that. "So what did you call about?"

"Can you make dinner tonight?"

Her heart stuttered almost as badly as her car had before the engine died. She was quite aware of the clerk's attention moving back and forth between her and the man behind her in line. They were the only two people in sight who didn't seem to be purchasing holiday items. "Tonight should be all right. I'll let Gram know that she'll be on her own—"

"Bring her along."

"I'm sure she'd like that." She handed over her cash to the clerk and moved out of the way with her two plastic bags while he paid for the dog food, which he hefted once again over his shoulder. "What time," she asked when they walked outside to the parking lot. "And where?"

"My parents' place. Where are you parked?" He angled that direction when she pointed. "I'll pick you up around six."

She eyed him. Overhead, the cloudless sky was an icy blue. There was a steady breeze that toyed with the dark hair falling across his forehead and, in the strong sunlight, she picked out even more strands of silver. "Are you sure you're ready to do this?" He didn't look as if he was. If anything, it appeared that he'd rather be on another continent than arranging this particular get-together.

"No." His lips twisted. "But that's not a reason to hold off any longer."

She had no comment for that. With every step forward, her certainty that she was doing the right thing seemed to take a step backward.

They reached her car and she stowed her purchases in the trunk alongside the pretty shopping bag holding the Irish wool sweater she'd bought for Kathleen at Classic Charms, and the piñata she'd picked up at the dime store.

She was ready to close the trunk when Ryan picked up the wire loop at the top of the castle-shaped piñata. "Looks like party stuff."

"It is. Seven girls from Chloe's class. This Saturday."

"Lucky you," he said drily, and let go of the wire.

She closed the trunk. "You can come," she said, even

though she wasn't entirely sure it was a good idea. "I should have told you that before."

"Eight seven-year-old girls?" He visibly shuddered.

"Chloe would love it."

"Now you're playing dirty."

That wasn't her intention. "Okay, so Chloe will probably be plenty busy with her little friends. I just didn't want you to think you weren't welcome."

With a shrug, he pulled the bag off his shoulder and stood it on the ground to lean against his leg.

She realized she was staring at the solid bulge of jean-clad thigh and quickly looked upward. The gaze she encountered was no less disturbing. Probably more.

"Your daughter is going to have relatives coming out of the woodwork once word gets out about her," he warned. "How's she going to take that?"

"She's your daughter, too," she said, though her throat tightened around the words. She was used to having total control where her daughter was concerned. But he was Chloe's father. Weren't his rights on a par with hers?

His lips tightened a little. He glanced around the parking lot that was only partially filled with cars. "All right. When she finds herself in the midst of a couple dozen relatives, how is *our* daughter going to handle it?"

It was the first time he'd verbally acknowledged Chloe as his and that's what should have struck her.

Instead, it was the intimacy in those words, *our daughter,* that had nervous energy ricocheting through her. Mallory wished that she could attribute it specifically to Chloe, but honesty made her admit at least to herself that it was the "our" part that made her knees feel shaky.

She squeezed the car keys in her hand, giving herself something else to focus on, even if it was only the discomfort of jagged-edged keys digging into her palm. "Chloe will be perfectly fine. She's a well-adjusted, caring and friendly child. There's no reason to think otherwise. You're the one with… issues."

"And I suppose you have a diagnosis?"

His deep voice was silky smooth and she realized that his tall, broad form was blocking the path to her car door. Instead of being alarmed though, the jolt that worked through her was distinctly…aroused.

Which was ridiculous.

They were standing in the parking lot of Shop-World. Who had their knees go weak over a man in such a place?

Foolish question. Dr. Mallory Keegan did.

"Maybe I would if I understood what your issues were," she countered, aiming for crisp and missing by a mile. "You know…everything about us. But we—" as in *I* "—know hardly anything about you."

"Everything?" He shook his head. "Not even close." He found her hand and lifted it, slowly prying open her fingers to reveal the reddening splotches. They were not quite welts, but they would have been with a little more time. "Shame," he tsked almost under his breath.

He slid the keys from her grasp and stole her breath right out of her body when he lifted her palm even higher and his breath—very, very warm in contrast to the thirty-some degree day—caressed her skin.

She knew she should pull her hand away. Curl her fingers up again. Do something, anything, but stand there and wait with agonizing anticipation for him to close even that breath-size space between his lips and her open, *offered,* palm.

She was a doctor, for pity's sake. Women's bodies and health issues were her particular field of expertise. She knew the science behind chemistry and sexual attraction. Knew the mechanics behind sex, period, and even though it had been a while, had at least a passing personal acquaintance with it.

But, oh heaven, she couldn't think of any science that could explain this mindless yearning.

And she almost whimpered when, instead of pressing his warm lips to her hand, he slid her palm along his jaw.

The abrading of the shadowy stubble there was almost worse than his lips would have been.

Worse. Better. What was the difference?

She felt like she was coming undone.

She swallowed, hard. "Ryan." It came out husky and thick. "What—" But she broke off, because she didn't even know what she wanted to say. If she wanted to say anything at all. "I thought you didn't want…this."

He still held her palm against his jaw. She could feel the working of a muscle beneath the pad of her index finger.

"I don't."

The stinging confirmation accomplished what her own willpower couldn't. The mesmerizing spell he seemed to have cast broke, leaving her feeling oddly dizzy as she easily tugged her hand free.

Had it been that easy all along?

Uncertainty dogged her as she sidestepped past him to the car door, only to realize that he still had her keys. She started to turn back, but he was already slipping the key into the door lock.

It was unnerving how quickly the man moved at times.

He unlocked the door, pulled it open and handed her the key. "I'll see you about six."

Her cheeks heated because the dinner plans had completely slipped her mind. Without looking at him, she nodded and pulled the door shut.

She watched in the mirror as he shouldered the massive bag of dog food again and, when he'd moved away from the rear of her car, she backed out and drove away, feeling as if the devil was at her heels.

* * *

"That was a delicious meal, Rebecca," Mallory said several hours later. She set the plates she'd helped clear from the table on the deeply colored granite counter next to the kitchen sink where the hospital chief—wearing an oddly incongruous "kiss the cook" apron over a pair of narrow black slacks and a pink sweater—stood rinsing dishes. "I don't know how you do it. I barely have the energy to heat leftovers in the microwave when I'm finished for the day."

"A roast is easy," Rebecca said blithely. She set the stack of plates from Mallory into the sink and directed the water over them. "I can't tell you how much this has meant to Sawyer and me," she said softly. She looked at the large window that was situated above the sink.

It was dark outside, but the outdoor lights shining over the wood deck that ran the entire width of the back of the house clearly illuminated the two men and the little girl who stood between them.

A ridiculously ugly dog with flopping ears and the name of Beowulf was chasing the stick that Ryan's father was tossing. He'd bounce through the snow that reached up to his belly, ferret out the stick and bounce his way back for a giggling hug from Chloe, rewarded with a sloppy lick over her face, and then bounce off again.

At least Mallory knew now who the dog food had been for; Ryan had had the bag in the back of his pickup truck when he'd picked them up.

The evening had been a total success if all Mallory considered was Chloe, and Ryan's parents. The elder Clays had seemed genuinely disappointed that Kathleen had had another commitment—a quilting circle that Mallory hadn't even been aware her grandmother had decided to join. But that disappointment hadn't really stood a chance against the sheer joy in their faces whenever they'd looked at Chloe.

Chloe who, after learning what their plans were for the evening, had asked Mallory again if Mr. Ryan was her boyfriend.

Mallory had denied it as certainly as she had the first time, though she was afraid her daughter hadn't believed a word of it. But she hadn't had time to deal with that, because Ryan had arrived then, and Chloe had merely sat between them on the truck ride over, beaming at both of them like some benevolent fairy godmother.

What *hadn't* been a success that evening was Ryan.

He might be standing outside there now with his father and his daughter, but his hands were shoved in his pockets and he carried the same air of remoteness around him that he'd assumed from the moment they'd walked through the front door of his parents' incredibly beautiful home.

Even Chloe had noticed his mood, giving him more than a few concerned looks through the meal.

When the concern in her daughter's face had started to slowly slide into hurt, Mallory had wanted to kick him.

Only good manners had controlled the uncharacteristically violent urge.

Fortunately, when Sawyer had suggested they let the dog out for a run, Chloe's face had brightened up again.

"I don't think Ryan is very happy about it." Mallory gave his mother an apologetic look.

Rebecca sighed a little and loaded the last dish in the dishwasher. She shut off the water faucet and dried her hands on her apron. "It's not Chloe," she assured.

"How can you be sure?" It was probably not the most tactful thing to ask. Rebecca *was* Ryan's mother.

"Because I saw him with both of you at the hospital," Rebecca reminded. "It's *not* Chloe. Ryan is…well, he's better since he's found you than he's been in months."

He hadn't found *them* so much as been hunted by her, Mallory thought.

"It's being here at the house where he grew up," Rebecca continued, unaware of the troubled turn of Mallory's mind. "Being with his family that still bothers him."

Rebecca's voice was calm and quiet, but Mallory could see the faint tremble in her slender fingers as she turned a beautifully artistic pecan pie this way and that on the counter before dipping the point of a sharp knife into the center and making quick work of the slices. "I know the what," she said. "I just don't know the why. Other than it has to do with that business that kept him away from us for so long." She pointed the knife at a glass-fronted cabinet behind Mallory. "Would you mind getting down the dessert plates?"

Mallory retrieved the small plates and Rebecca began dishing up the slices. "What *was* that business?" On one hand, she felt she was going around Ryan's back for information that he should be the one to provide. But on the other hand, she badly needed to know what she was dealing with.

For Chloe's sake, she excused. It wasn't untrue.

Nor was it the entire truth.

Rebecca's hands paused over the pie slices. "I wish I knew," she sighed. "My son was one man when he left us nearly five years ago. He was another man when he returned nine months ago." Her head tilted a little. "But no matter what happened in those years between, he's still my son." She slipped the last slice onto a plate and when she looked up her smile was steady though her eyes were a shade too bright. "He's alive and he's home. And now we have his daughter in our life, too. Next to Ryan's return, it's the best Christmas present any of us could ever have."

"I'm sorry that I'm not ready to tell Chloe, yet."

But Rebecca just smiled softly. "I've told you that is your decision, Mallory. Please don't let that worry you. We're going to love Chloe no matter what, and when you do tell her we're her family, too—well, then it will just make something wonderful that much more complete. Now here." She handed two plates to Mallory. "Take them into the family room if you would, and I'll call them inside. Do you think Chloe would like ice cream instead of pie? Or *with* her pie?"

Mallory let out a breath. "I think she wouldn't care if it were yogurt on cardboard after getting to play with Beowulf like she has."

Rebecca's laughter followed her out of the kitchen.

In the spacious family room, there was a fire burning low in the wide stone fireplace. She set the plates on the large square coffee table situated in the center of a massive leather sectional before moving over to the tall fir Christmas tree beside a wide window. The tree was studded with so many ornaments that only as she got closer to look at it did she realize many were as homemade as the ones yet to be hung on their own tree.

She smiled a little at the school pictures pasted in the center of glittery stars; some craft projects didn't change no matter what decade it was. From the tree that already had several gaily wrapped packages tucked beneath, she moved toward the fireplace mantel to study the collection of frames clustered among a stunning flocked pine garland. She couldn't help lowering her head toward the garland and inhaling the crisp, green scent as her gaze traveled over the delicate beauty of the nearly translucent, ivory glass bulbs threaded among the garland, to the photographs.

Sawyer and Rebecca, decades younger, arm in arm as they looked at each other so plainly in love. A young, grinning Ryan wearing a football uniform with a trophy in one hand and a football in the other. Courtney, impossibly lovely in a formal gown, probably a prom dress. And then the photos of the four of them, all together as a family.

She picked up one photograph that was tucked almost in the back of the others. More recent, this one. Sawyer and Rebecca looking very much as they did now, though Sawyer's hair hadn't gone entirely gray, yet. Courtney was no longer a schoolgirl and Ryan was clearly a man, right down to the navy whites he was wearing.

Her throat felt tight as her thumb hovered over his handsome image, not touching the glass lest she leave smudges behind.

"Who are you?" she murmured to herself.

"Maybe you should have asked that before you brought Chloe to Weaver," he said behind her.

She pressed the frame to her breast and whirled. "I thought you were still outside. Where's Chloe?"

"My mother is showing her where Beowulf sleeps."

She was still clutching the photograph and she quickly replaced it. "And your father?"

"Outside stealing a smoke." He reached around her to pull out the picture she'd just so carefully replaced. "My mother doesn't approve," he added absently.

She knew that Ryan smoked on occasion, though he'd never done so around her or Chloe. Yet he hadn't chosen to stay outside with his father and share that time. "I don't approve, either," she said. "Shortens your life."

His lips twisted a little. "Sometimes that's the idea. My sister was the homecoming queen at the high school here four years running," he went on before her frown could turn into a comment. "She's still one of the prettiest things I've ever seen."

"But you hardly seemed to want to talk to her the day we were at the hospital with Chloe." The fact that his aloof demeanor throughout the evening shifted into something even harder, colder, didn't stop her runaway tongue. "You hardly want to talk to any of your family members, from what I can tell."

He pushed the picture frame back on the mantel, dislodging one of the delicate glass bulbs. It rolled off the mantel, but he shot out a hand, catching it before it could fall to the hardwood floor. "Leave it alone, Doc."

But her runaway tongue wasn't finished. "I can't."

"Why? I talk to Chloe. Isn't that what you wanted?"

"Of course, but—"

"What goes on between me and my family won't affect how they feel about Chloe."

"I know that." She'd seen it for herself, hadn't she?

"Then why the hell does it matter to you?"

"Because you matter to me!" She stared as the words dissolved into the silence around them.

The fire crackled softly. Deep in the house she could hear the high pitch of Chloe's indistinct words and the lower murmur of Rebecca's, the sound of a door closing.

"Because you matter, Ryan," she said. More softly. More deliberately.

His expression was still remote; his eyes were anything but. "Because of Chloe."

"Because of—" *me* "—all of us," she finally settled on. Judiciously. Cowardly.

He exhaled sharply. "Chloe didn't know me before. They did."

Before he'd been gone.

She suddenly felt as if she were standing in the center of an ocean of very thin, very fragile ice and if she reached out to touch him the way she badly wanted to do, they'd both go crashing through it. "What happened during those years you were gone, Ryan?"

"Mom," Chloe propelled herself into the room, barely stopping in time to keep from smashing into Mallory's side. "Dr. Rebecca says I can play with Beowulf whenever I want!" Her face was full of glee. "We can come again, right?"

Mallory nodded and managed a smile for her daughter. "Yes. You can come again."

She was pleased for her daughter's sake.

But one look at Ryan's face put an end to her burgeoning hope that—before Chloe had interrupted them—he'd been on the verge of actually answering her.

Chapter Eleven

"If this is a birthday party, why are we hanging Christmas decorations instead of balloons?"

Mallory handed another ornament to Ryan, who was using a stepstool to reach the top branches of the tree.

It was Saturday. The day of Chloe's seventh birthday. And in a short while, there would be eight little girls, including Chloe, probably racing around like terrors, from what Mallory remembered of the birthday parties from when she and Cassie were young.

But for three days now, ever since the dinner at his parents' home, instead of being preoccupied by Chloe's looming birthday party, Mallory had found herself preoccupied by the man who was Chloe's father.

Or rather, the mystery of the man who was Chloe's father. She was no closer to understanding Ryan than she had been at his parents' home.

He'd turned to hang the deep blue pear-shaped ornament

on the tree and she absently plucked another from the box to hand to him. "We have to finish decorating it now, because Chloe fully expects a decorated tree for her birthday."

"Until she was four, she believed it was all part of the celebration for *her* birthday," Kathleen added. She set a tray of crown-shaped cookies topped with lilac frosting on the table next to the packing box, then stood back with her hands on her hips to survey the tree. "Finest tree we've ever had," she determined.

"And the balloons come next," Mallory finished, warning. She dragged her gaze from the breadth of Ryan's shoulders that were clearly delineated beneath the long-sleeved charcoal sweater he wore as he turned to hang the next ornament, to look at the pile of party decorations they still had to deal with before Chloe's guests started arriving.

Not surprisingly, Chloe had accomplished what Mallory had not. Ryan hadn't been able to turn her down when she'd beseeched him to be there for her party.

And right now the birthday girl was upstairs in her room, debating which outfit to wear. She'd gone reluctantly just a few minutes ago only because Mallory—from long experience—knew that on some occasions, these things could take time.

Chloe was, after all, female. Even if only seven. And she had at least a dozen purple-hued outfits from which to choose.

Mallory realized that Ryan's long-fingered, square-palmed hand was extended, waiting for another ornament. She reached blindly into the box, grabbing whatever her fingers encountered first, and dropped it in his palm.

It was yellow, shaped like a rattle, and it said "Chloe's first Christmas" on it.

Cassie had ordered it specially from a catalog while she was pregnant, even though Chloe hadn't been due until January.

Mallory's throat suddenly felt tight, but for the first time the ache she felt wasn't sharp as a scalpel. It was duller.

Muted. And the poignancy of watching Ryan study it silently before squeezing her hand and gently hanging the ornament on the tree had her heart melting. Unnerved, she quickly pulled the last two ornaments out of the box. She didn't look at Ryan as she handed them to him, and as soon as she had done so, she plucked the square packing box off the table to carry out to the kitchen. She'd find a closet somewhere to store it in later.

"That's it? What about the tree topper?"

"We don't have one," Kathleen said as she reached for the empty box. "I'll take care of this, dear. You worry about all that." She gestured toward the rest of the decorations that were of the more traditional birthday variety.

"Thanks, Gram." Mallory was going to get her mind on Chloe and *off* her father, and that was that. She sat down on the floor and tore open two bags of balloons. Twelve purple. Twelve lime-green. It was eye-popping and Chloe's favorite combination. And with two dozen balloons to blow up, she was strongly wishing that she'd thought to rent a helium tank or even an air pump. Resigned, she lifted the first balloon to her mouth and started to fill it the old-fashioned way.

"Have something against tree toppers I should know about?" Ryan edged the cookie tray over to one side and sat down on the coffee table. He picked up a balloon, stretching it between his fingers.

She shook her head but kept blowing.

"Your cheeks are turning red," he observed.

Successfully making her feel more self-conscious.

She lowered the balloon, pinching the top of it between her fingers so as not to lose her hard-blown air. "You showed up this morning saying you wanted to help. So put your comments inside the balloons," she suggested wryly, and resumed blowing.

He smiled faintly, but merely continued stretching the

rubbery balloon. "I would have been there yesterday while she got her cast, but I got hung up out at J.D.'s."

Studying the fatness of the balloon was easier than studying him and she deemed it full enough to tie off the end before adding a short curly piece of ribbon to it. When all of the balloons were filled and tied off in a similar way, she'd hang those ribbons from a wider one strung over the dining room table where Chloe's nauseatingly purple birthday cake sat center stage. "I never expected you to drop everything in your life to spend all of your time with Chloe," she assured him. If anything, given the way he'd learned about Chloe's existence, Mallory was surprised and a little—or a lot—affected by his general willingness ever since the E.R. incident to be around Chloe as much as he had been.

But she would have bet her little finger that he'd been perfectly happy to have any reason to avoid again going to the hospital, where he might possibly run into his sister or his mother.

"Had to help Jake move Latitude back to J.D.'s."

The names were familiar only because J. D. Clay herself had been in Mallory's office that week for an ultrasound and had talked the entire while about Jake, and the injured racehorse they were trying to save. It was certainly not because Ryan had been particularly talkative about what all he did for his cousin and her horse-boarding business.

He's talking now, a small voice inside her reminded.

"Did that go well?" What she knew about racehorses would have fit on the head of a pin.

"As well as it could, considering he has casts on two legs now."

"That's good." She wanted to keep him talking. But she was also aware of the clock ticking merrily along. She picked up another balloon, green this time, and blew it up.

After a moment he blew up his balloon, too, doing it in

easily half the time that she took. He tied it off and handed it to her when she'd finished with her own.

"We always had an angel on the top of our tree." He'd glanced up at the tree that—even if she did say so herself, looked particularly wonderful this year—as if the bare top was nagging at him. "Looked sorta like Courtney."

The green balloon spit out from her fingers before she could wrap the ribbon around the end, and she scrambled after it before it could bounce toward the tree. Experience had long ago taught her that spiky Christmas tree bristles, no matter how fresh, were not compatible with filled balloons.

"Must have been a very pretty angel, then." She captured the balloon and sat down with it again, rapidly attaching the curly ribbon. "Would have to be to look like your sister."

He just picked up another balloon and filled it with only a couple of long, strong exhales. For every one balloon she filled, he did two. And in shorter order than she'd dared hope for, all of the balloons were full and he seemed willing enough to position the entire mess of ribbons and balloons where she indicated.

And then Chloe came down, clapping her hands together in appreciation for their efforts. "It's the bestest tree we've ever had. I wish everyone could have a tree just like this."

It was impossible not to smile about the happiness radiating from Chloe's face, and Mallory found herself looking over her daughter's head to Ryan. He, too, was actually smiling.

Not as widely as Chloe. Not even as widely as Mallory. But it was a smile.

And then his gaze met Mallory's, and the world seemed to close in around them. Not because she saw the horribly frequent hollowness there that made her heart ache; not because she saw the sizzling flare that made her blood heat. Neither were there. What *was* there looked like contentment. Simple pleasure. Logically, she knew it could be just an echo of the happy emotion casting off Chloe like a fisherman's net, but something other than logic insisted otherwise.

She felt the edges of her own smile tremble a little. "Okay." She clapped her own hands together if only to break the spell she kept falling under where Ryan was concerned. "Christmas tree, check. Balloons and birthday cake, check. Birthday girl—" she picked Chloe up by the waist and kissed her nose "—check."

Then she quickly set her down. "You are growing, my dear." Getting taller every day. Would she be tall like Ryan and his sister? Considering Chloe already looked so much like Ryan it was a wonder people hadn't figured out their relationship simply by seeing them together, Mallory supposed it was pretty likely that her daughter would also inherit some of his height. "You'll probably be taller than me one day," she told her.

"That won't take much," Ryan said drily and Chloe giggled.

"Hey. Good things can come in shorter packages," Mallory defended humorously.

Ryan's eyes seemed to skip down her body, leaving puddles of heat in their wake. "Unquestionably."

"Mom, do you like my outfit?"

Focusing on her daughter gave her time to collect herself. "Very nice," she approved. Chloe's lavender T-shirt made her eyes seem bluer than ever, and her purple jeans were her newest pair, complete with a line of sparkling stitching right down the sides—that matched the purple cast on her arm. She'd even brushed her hair and slid on a shiny purple hair band that held it back from her face.

"Then can I open my presents?"

Mallory shook her head. "Presents after cake. Even the ones from Grammy and me."

"But—"

"Maybe one," Ryan suggested, drawing both of their surprised attention. "I got her something." He looked vaguely diffident, suddenly. "Maybe she could open that one now."

Chloe clasped her hands. "Oh, please please please."

Chloe's melodramatics, Mallory could have withstood. But the hint of vulnerability that was completely at odds with Ryan's usual demeanor?

The way her heart was squeezing with tenderness inside her was just one indication that her resistance to *that* was thoroughly extinct. "Okay." Chloe immediately cheered. "Just Ryan's gift, though, Chloe," she cautioned. "And then we're going to help Gram, and make sure everything is ready for your guests. That's part of being a good host."

Chloe was nodding, bouncing on her heels as she tilted her head back to look up at Ryan. "What is it?"

"If I told you, it wouldn't be a surprise." He gestured to the couches. "Wait here. Inside and away from the window. Your mom has to help me bring it inside."

"Bring *what* inside?" Mallory asked cautiously once they'd pulled on their coats and were outside on the step. She looked toward his truck parked at the curb, but couldn't see anything unusual in the bed of it.

"I know you're not going to be thrilled," he started off, with no hint of apology in his voice, though her stomach clutched anyway. "But she obviously wants one."

She closed her eyes for a second, only to open them again quickly for fear that he'd conjure out of thin air what she was strongly hoping he wouldn't. "Please tell me you didn't get her a puppy."

But she could see by his expression that was exactly what he'd done.

"He's ten weeks old," Ryan said. "Weaned and house-trained already."

She wasn't sure if she was more dismayed or irritated. "Great. Then *you* won't have to worry about him piddling in *your* house," she said. What if Ryan's attentiveness didn't last? What if fatherhood wasn't for him after all? It had been only a week since he'd learned of Chloe's existence. "Don't you think you should have run this by me first?"

"He *will* be at my house," he countered.

All the wind she'd been pumping into her righteous sails fizzled. The sails collapsed, leaving her blinking at him. "*You* have a house."

His lips tightened a little. "Yes, Doc, even a derelict, mostly unemployed handyman that I am, I have a house."

She wasn't going to let him make her feel bad, because that hadn't been what she'd been thinking at all. "But you live at the Sleep Tite."

From his pocket, he pulled a key ring containing a very few keys. "As of this morning—" he jangled one key in particular "—I live over there." He turned and pointed at the house diagonally across the street from hers. "And don't get your panties in a knot. I didn't buy it. I rented it."

It was a wonder her jaw didn't hit the cement step on which they were standing. "You rented that house." She seemed incapable of doing anything but repeating every point he was trying to make. She eyed the house in question.

It was smaller than the one she was renting but looked quite a bit newer. And maybe it didn't say much about her as a neighbor, but she hadn't even realized the place was vacant, much less available for rent.

"But…why?"

"Because it's available and because it's close." He exhaled so sharply that his breath was a visible stream in the cold air. "Though God knows *that's* probably going to bite me on the butt," he muttered.

She was supposed to be a fairly intelligent person, wasn't she? So why was she having such difficulty comprehending anything that he was saying? "Why?"

"Living across the street from you?" He stepped off the porch. "I might as well set up camp right inside the fire."

His tone was hardly complimentary. "Nobody asked you to live across the street from me," she returned, stung. "So why *are* you?"

He gave her a look. "What good is a mutt for Chloe if she can't see him when she wants? Now, are you going to help me get him over here before this place is crawling with miniature women, or not?"

Of course his unexpected change of digs was because of Chloe. His decision still had her completely thrown. Yet she found herself falling into step behind him, though she had to practically skip to keep up with him. "You do realize that you're going to have this…this dog even when *we* go back to New York." He was an intelligent man. Surely he knew that. "My leave of absence isn't indefinite. They are expecting me back. You and I will work out a fair visitation where Chloe's concerned, naturally, but I never intended that to include a dog."

He stopped in the middle of the narrow street and turned to face her. "Fair according to whom?"

She stared at him, stunned. "Where is this coming from? Only a week ago you couldn't wait to run away from the idea that Chloe might be yours."

"Now it's *might* be? Thought you were so damn sure she was."

She felt ridiculous tears sting behind her eyes. She wasn't even certain what they were disagreeing about or how easily they'd gone from companionably blowing up balloons to…this. "I *am* sure." She jabbed her finger into his chest. "And so are you!"

He caught her hand, twisting it to the side. He wasn't hurting her. He was just…completely controlling her ability to move a single inch. "If you didn't want me to get involved in her life in any way, you shouldn't have brought her here to

Weaver." He released her and turned on his heel, continuing across the street.

Wondering when she'd lost such complete control of the situation, she scrambled after him, the lapels of her coat flapping loosely, catching up to him only when he stopped long enough to open the front door of the house.

The second he did, she could hear a high-pitched yipping coming from inside.

She wasn't one to yell, but that's exactly what she found herself wanting to do. Yell. And pound on something.

Like his wide, wide back.

She curled her fingers into her palms and followed him inside, nearly slamming the door shut behind her. "Is that what you'd have preferred? That you never learned you even had a daughter? Never had someone who could sneak beneath that precious, almighty wall you want to keep built up around yourself?"

He stopped dead in his tracks again, turning so fast on his heel to face her that she gasped.

And she cried outright when his hands slid around her waist and she found herself pinned against the door that she, herself, had so angrily shut. "What do you think you're doing?"

His grip didn't lessen one iota. He stepped closer until she felt every unforgiving inch of him, from heart to hip, branded against her. "I told you before, it's not Chloe I have a problem with."

She lifted her chin, desperately ignoring the overwhelmingly masculine pressure of him. And her much-too-eager feminine reaction. "Right. *I'm* the problem. And this—" her voice dripped with hard-won disdain "—is the way you're solving it. By…manhandling me."

He gave a bark of laughter that was thoroughly devoid of amusement and succeeded only in pressing his chest even more squarely against her breasts. "Doc, of all the manhandling I've dreamed about where you're concerned, very *little* of it was done vertically."

Her cheeks went hot.

She was furious. He was none too happy, either.

But he was aroused and, heaven help her, so was she.

And they were both aware of it.

The puppy was still yapping, the incessant canine cries blending into the all-encompassing chaos that seemed to fill her head. "Stop dreaming about me."

Of all the things she could have—*should* have—said, that's what came out?

She wanted the earth to swallow her whole.

"Believe me." His jaw was so tight it was practically white. "If I could, I would."

Humiliation was the perfect topping to her sundae of frustration.

He hissed out an oath. "Don't go crying on me."

"I assure you I won't." The scathing tone didn't magically make the moisture blurring her vision disappear, though she wished it would.

His jaw canted slightly to one side. Then the other. "I can't be what you want, Mallory."

"I don't want anything from you!"

"Bull. You want a father for Chloe."

Add another helping of humiliation. Her love for Chloe was woven into her soul. So how on God's green earth could she keep forgetting that everything that transpired between her and Ryan involved her daughter?

His physical attraction to Mallory was merely an unwelcome inconvenience to him.

"You think you *can't* be her father so your answer to that is to give her a puppy that she's only going to have to leave behind in a few months?"

"I can't be a father in name only," he corrected. "Did you

even really want to find her father, Mallory? Or were you only looking for a face and a name to fill in the blanks in that baby book you've got on the shelf in your bedroom? Then you could take the book back with you all to New York and everything will be hunky-dory?"

It struck uncomfortably close to the truth, she realized. "You've been snooping in my bedroom?"

He gave her a look. "Chloe showed it to me. Just because you're not home every evening doesn't mean that I haven't been over there."

"I've had emergencies at the hospital," she said, temper quickly puffing air into those sails again. Did he know how torn she felt whenever her career had to take her attention away from her daughter? Did he know how she worried that she was shortchanging Chloe for the sake of her own needs? "I'm a doctor. It's what I do. And it's how I can afford to keep a roof over my family's head! For pity's sake, Ryan. You of all people should know those are demands that can't be ignored. And I've only had two emergencies this week!"

"And how many do you get back in New York?"

Her lips parted, but the words got stuck in her throat.

After what seemed an eternity, the fight went right out of her. Her shoulders sagged. "Too many," she said. Her voice was husky. Her emotions beat.

Somehow his hands had gone from her waist to her hips and she hadn't even been aware of it. But she was aware now. "Ryan—" But she broke off. She didn't know what she wanted to say.

She felt his fingers flex. "Living in the fire," he murmured. And lowered his head.

Chapter Twelve

Ryan saw the startled widening of Mallory's amber eyes in the moment before his mouth found hers.

If she'd protested, he'd have stopped.

But he'd known she wouldn't, and he was right.

She tasted just as sweetly dangerous as she had the first time he'd kissed her.

But that kiss had been brief. Hard. Fast.

This time…this time, he took his time.

Exploring the shape of her lips that had distracted him from the moment he'd first laid eyes on her. Delving into the softness that before he'd barely tested.

And Mallory was more than accommodating.

Her head angled against him, her lips parting, tongue glancing, flirting, dancing away and then back again.

He wanted to devour her. He wanted to savor her.

Mostly, he wanted.

Her.

He could have blamed his ravaging hunger on how long it had been since he'd been with a woman, but he'd given up lying to himself when he'd finally faced the truth that he couldn't bring down Krager.

His hunger now was all about Mallory.

Only she could appease it.

If making love to her just once would put the dragon inside him back to sleep, he'd damn the consequences and find the nearest bed.

His hands gripped her hips. Her legs parted, allowing him to step even closer into the warmth of her body.

For that matter, who needed a bed?

Her hands were behind his neck. Her fingers clutched his hair, his head and soft, maddening sounds curled from her throat.

For the first time in his life, though, just once was not going to be enough.

Not nearly enough.

And he'd been around long enough to know that his newfound daughter's mother wasn't the kind of woman to burn up the sheets over and over again with a man without…entanglements.

He was a lot closer to forty than not, and he'd gone his entire life without that sort of tangling. He wasn't about to start now, when the only thing he had to offer was an empty soul and a mountain of regret. Especially with the woman who was raising his daughter.

"Wait." Her mouth tore away from his. She pressed her forehead to his shoulder. The scent of her hair teased him. Fresh. Like a summer day.

Grapefruit, he realized, and wondered how on earth it could smell so damn enticing that all he wanted to do was bury his face in her hair.

Her breaths were still shuddering through them both. "Wait. I…we…can't do this."

Isn't that what he'd been trying to convince himself of?

So why in hell did he want to tip her head back again and taste her mouth; explore the smooth column of her throat; discover the warmth of her skin in the valley between her breasts—

He yanked his hands away from her hips, setting her feet on the floor. "Damn straight we can't," he muttered grimly. He stepped back and turned away from her, though he could see the way she swayed unsteadily, slapping an arm out to her side against the door for balance.

"Right."

Even the sound of that single, breathless word made him want more. Made him want to know whether she'd moan softly when he took her, if she'd make those low, purring sounds in her throat as he drove her closer to the edge. He wanted to know if she'd cry out when they blasted beyond it.

"The party," she added, still panting. "Chloe's waiting."

The reminder should have been as effective as a bucket of ice water in cooling him off. It did a piss-poor job, though.

The puppy was still caterwauling from the kennel cage where Ryan had placed it in the completely empty dining room early that morning.

Without looking at Mallory—because doing that would probably only exacerbate his dilemma—he went out to the dining room and opened the metal crate.

The mutt leaped straight up into Ryan's arms, shaking with sheer excitement, slathering anything he could reach with his sloppy wet tongue. He cradled the dog's little round belly in his palm and carried him out the back door to the yard.

The yard was small but, unlike Mallory's place, it was fenced. He set the pup on his feet at the bottom of the porch stairs and he immediately tore off for the fence line. His small body would have been practically invisible in the snow if not for his chestnut markings.

And even though he was focused on the dog, Ryan could

have been deaf and blind and still known when Mallory came up behind him, because every cell in his body went on alert.

Fortunately, she didn't brush even a sleeve against him as she stepped around him onto the porch to watch the puppy's antics as he popped in and out of the snow. "I suppose I should be grateful that Chloe didn't tell you she wanted a horse." She sounded more like her ordinary, composed self, albeit resigned.

Didn't do a damn thing for the unrelenting tightness in his jeans.

He closed his hand around the metal railing that guarded the edge of the porch. It was either that, or chance reaching for her again, and his self-control had already reached its limit. "A horse would have been easier to come by than the hairy beast, there. My uncle has a horse farm, for one thing. And my cousin and I used to talk about going into horse breeding, ourselves."

Mallory gave him an alarmed glance over her shoulder. "Don't you even think about it."

"Christmas *is* in less than two weeks."

"Ryan—"

"Relax. I'm kidding." If Chloe was interested in horses, she didn't have to own one to have easy access to one.

Mallory's mouth snapped closed. She looked back toward the dog. "Good thing."

"Never got much past the talking with Axel, anyway." Mostly because Ryan had been chasing around the world trying to destroy a monster. "He and Evan are having some success at it, though." He knew he was rambling. Keeping his mouth busy with something other than her mouth.

"Evan?"

"Taggart. The veterinarian. A friend. Married to my cousin, Leandra." He nodded toward the puppy, whose curious nose had led him back to the porch steps. "He arranged the mutt."

She scooped the dog up in her arms. "I may be just an ignorant doctor, Ryan, but I know this is no mutt." Her finger smoothed over the dog's finely shaped head. "What is he? A spaniel of some sort?"

"Cavalier King Charles."

"Even the name sounds expensive! Was he?"

"He's a gift, Doc. You're not supposed to ask about the cost of gifts."

"In other words, he *was* expensive." She looked bewildered. "Chloe doesn't need pricey gifts from you, Ryan. All she cares about is your time and, even when she knows the truth, that's not going to change."

"You think this is some attempt at winning her affection?"

"What else would prompt you to spend money you can probably ill afford?"

He almost laughed. "Mallory, you're so far off you're not even in the ballpark."

"You don't have to be sensitive. *I* couldn't afford to blow money on an expensive dog, either."

He could buy a hundred dogs like this one and not even feel the effects. That's what happened when you earned the kind of money he had and for as long as he had. Add in the fact that working numbers came as naturally to him as breathing and he'd amassed a fortune even before he'd turned thirty. He'd also realized that no amount of money was worth losing your soul, but by then it was too late. "Let me worry about my finances. I'm not exactly on the dole."

He wondered if Mallory was even aware of the way she was rubbing her cheek against the puppy's silky head. Her eyes were almost the same shade as the dog's brown spots.

And getting caught up in the drugging warmth of that gaze again was not going to get them across the street where a seven-year-old girl and her eighty-year-old great-grandmother could provide very adequate chaperoning.

He rubbed the dog's nose. "Evan just found the pooch two days ago. He wasn't even sure he could get him here to Weaver by today. I would have told you, Mallory, if I'd have had a chance."

She didn't look convinced. But she didn't look as if she still wanted to draw and quarter him, either.

He also knew that was probably due more to holding that damnably cute, squirming little puppy than it was to him, personally.

But he wasn't proud.

He'd take what he could get.

He realized he was staring at her fingers as they stroked slowly over the dog's silky ears, and he yanked open the storm door gesturing for her to go inside.

"I've got a leash for him but figured Chloe ought to be the one to pick out anything else. If she doesn't find what she wants in town, there's a good-size pet store in Braden. We could drive over tomorrow, maybe." He reached into the kennel cage and pulled out a brilliant purple blanket. "It's a baby blanket," he said, feeling self-conscious. "Tara had it at her shop. It was the only thing purple that I could find. The mutt likes it."

Mallory stood stock-still in the dining room next to the cage. She was still cradling the puppy. The sunlight slanted through the tall windows, shining across her hair, making it glimmer as though it had been dusted with gold.

He decided in that moment that he had a seriously bad case of starvation when his brain conjured such poetic notions.

"You really care about her." Her voice was little more than a whisper.

He shrugged, feeling uneasy. "What did you expect?"

She looked uncertain. Vulnerable. "I don't know," she admitted after a moment. "It just wasn't…this."

He was pretty damn curious what exactly "this" meant.

"I don't know what you think the job description for daddy entails, Doc. I'm only doing what it seems like I ought to be doing. It's not like discovering a daughter was on my calendar this month." He had no experience being a father. But he'd had two of them—good ones—who'd set an example. He figured he'd fall miles short—he had in every other way—but he was doing what he could. "If you don't like it, then—"

"No," she interrupted quickly. "No, no. I do. Too much, really." She exhaled. "I'm making a mess of this. I know. I'm sorry." She brushed her cheek against the puppy's head and the little beast's eyes rolled in ecstasy. "Here." She settled the dog in the crook of Ryan's arm and tucked the blanket around him. "You show him to Chloe. He's from you, after all."

He eyed her, looking for some catch and finding nothing at all in her face but an odd expression that he couldn't interpret. "You're not mad anymore?"

Her lips twisted wryly. "You're going to make her day. Her *year*. It would be pretty churlish of me not to realize that, even if the finer details are not exactly worked out."

"Life happens with or without the details all being dotted and crossed."

"*Now* you're sounding like Gram."

"Because I've learned just how little there is that we can control?"

She tied the belt of her coat around her slender waist. "All the more reason to keep control of those things that we *can*." She headed toward the foyer and the front door, obviously taking in the complete lack of furnishings. "You don't even have a chair to sit on."

"So? I just got the key this morning. Right before I picked up the pooch. And furniture's easy enough to come by."

"In Weaver?" She looked disbelieving.

"Even in little old Weaver." He smiled faintly. "Darlin', I've got family coming out of the woodwork around here. There's always furniture sitting unused in someone's basement or attic. There's only one thing I'll want new, anyway."

"What's that?"

He reached around her to open the door. Which again brought him close enough to smell the fragrance of her hair. "A bed."

Given that Mallory was a trained physician, Ryan found it amazingly easy to rattle her.

A rosy blush spread across her high cheekbones. Dipped down her neck.

And probably beyond.

Clearly, rattling her was a double-edged sword because he'd just sliced himself right open with want, all over again.

If she was aware of that particular fact, she managed to hide it, though, by angling her chin upward and sailing through the doorway without sparing him another glance.

The dog whimpered softly and gave Ryan a slow, wet lick across his hand.

Sympathy from a dog.

"Let's just hope Chloe doesn't want to name you Princess," he told the puppy, and pulled the door shut to follow Mallory back across the street.

Chloe was beside herself with impatience by the time he and Mallory crossed the street and found her in the living room. "*What took you so long?* Grammy and I finished hanging up the Christmas stockings but I've been waiting and waiting...."

She spotted the brown-and-white head above the purple blanket and her words dried up.

The growing wonder in her bright blue eyes was enough to make Ryan's chest feel tight.

He damn near jumped out of his skin when Mallory settled her hand on his arm. There was a soft look in her eyes, as if she knew exactly what he was feeling.

Hell, maybe she did.

Up to now, she'd had Chloe's previous six birthdays all to herself. Ample opportunities to learn how one little girl can reach inside you and grab hold of your heart.

Even one as walled off as his.

"Is that—" Chloe didn't seem capable of finishing the question, probably fearing that if she did, the magic of the moment might evaporate.

Mallory's gaze met his. She gave an imperceptible nod. Encouraging him even though, only minutes ago, she'd been fit to strangle him.

He bent his knees, crouching down closer to Chloe's level.

"Oh my gosh," she breathed, and the puppy, either sensing freedom or a soul mate, scrabbled out from the swaddling blanket and leaped to the floor. His tiny paws slipped and slid on the hardwood floor as he aimed straight for Chloe's outstretched hands.

"Oh my gosh," she said again. And again as she sat right down on her rear. The puppy climbed onto her lap, planted his tiny paws on her chest and proceeded to lick her to death. "I *love* him." Her whisper was fervent. "Oh, Mr. Ryan, he's the very best birthday present in the whole world. Mommy, do I really get to keep him?"

Ryan cleared his throat, ready to explain that the dog should stay at his place, but Mallory's hand touched him again. This time resting on his shoulder.

"Yes," she answered. Her voice sounded as thick as his tongue felt. "You really get to keep him."

"Good gracious," Kathleen exclaimed, coming into the room to see the fuss. She was holding a punch bowl filled with pink-colored punch. "Would you look at that! My Gretchen had a puppy just like that when she was a wee girl. That was your mama's mama, Chloe."

"Isn't he wonderful?" Despite her cast, Chloe was doing

her best to hold on to the excited puppy as he practically climbed up to her shoulders.

"Indeed he is," Kathleen agreed. Her eyes were dancing as she retreated with the bowl once again.

"A puppy is a big responsibility," Mallory said. "You have to make sure he has food and water—"

"I will, I will—"

"And that he goes outside to go potty—"

"I will, I will!" She twisted around onto her knees, then awkwardly stood up, still holding his squirming body. "Oh, thank you, Mommy." She wrapped her other arm around Mallory's hips.

Mallory smoothed back Chloe's hair. "You're welcome, but you need to thank Ryan. The puppy is from him."

Chloe's hug transferred to him. "Oh, thank you, Mr. Ryan. I love him. And I love you."

He figured the words were just the enthusiasm of an ecstatic seven-year-old. But she was looking up at him with such a wealth of joy he wasn't sure he'd ever recover from it. "Maybe just Ryan would do," he suggested gruffly.

"Maybe something else would do better," Mallory said, her voice soft. Husky. Her gaze glanced off his. "Chloe, there's something you should know about Ryan."

Alarm shot down his spine. Was she just going to blurt it out now? No preparation. Right before Chloe's party?

Springing it on him the way he'd sprung the puppy on her? Only this was a helluva lot more life changing. "Mallory—"

But Chloe just giggled, looking up at him. "I know one thing about him. He's standing under the mistletoe. And so are you."

Obviously disconcerted by her daughter's observation, Mallory looked up where Chloe was pointing above their heads. A sprig of mistletoe, tied with a red ribbon, hung from the center of the doorway. "Where did that come from?"

"Grammy and I hung it up. She hadda stand on a chair,

though." Laughter bubbled out of her when the puppy leaped from her arms only to run in circles around her feet. "She says if you stand under it with someone else, you gotta kiss."

The look Mallory slanted toward him was startled and just as wary as he felt.

He solved the matter simply enough by scooping Chloe up into his arms. He held her between him and Mallory and she smiled faintly, obviously on to his solution.

The dog was going mad, yapping even more excitedly around their feet. Ryan kissed Chloe on one cheek.

Mallory kissed her on the other. "There. Now we're all kissed."

Chloe just rolled her eyes. "No, we're not." Managing to wrap her casted arm around Ryan's neck, she tugged. "You got to kiss each *other.*"

"Chloe." Mallory chided with laughter that was plainly nervous, at least to his ears. "We really should be getting ready for your guests. They'll start arriving soon. And you need to think of a name for your puppy."

"I got a name already," she said promptly. "And Grammy says we're already ready for my party. All we need are the people."

Ryan managed not to smile at the consternation that crossed Mallory's face before she could smooth it away. She leaned over Chloe, stretching up to plant a quick peck on Ryan's jaw. "Okay. There."

Chloe's gaze slid to his, clearly disgusted with her mother's attempt. She obviously expected him to do better.

Problem was, both he and Mallory knew just how much better they *could* do.

But not with a manipulative, no matter how sweet, little girl situated between them.

He'd faced down life-threatening situations with less caution, for God's sake.

He thrust his hand through the rich, soft waves guarding

Mallory's neck and tugged her forward. Pressed his lips to hers and let her go just as quickly.

He didn't look again at her as he set Chloe on the floor, but he managed to catch the speculative look on her grandmother's face since Kathleen had obviously witnessed at least the last part of the scene.

He almost felt seventeen again and had been caught kissing Anya Johannson in the backseat of his mother's car when Anya had been just fourteen.

He'd been grounded for a month and assigned to his grandfather, Squire, who'd had plenty of opinions about what kind of behavior was expected of a Clay.

"Chloe." Mallory seemed just as intent on not looking at him as she adjusted the headband in Chloe's hair an inch. "What's the name you picked out for the puppy?"

"Abercrombie."

It was so far from anything Ryan could have expected, he couldn't help but laugh. "Where'd you come up with a name like that?"

"Abercrombie," Mallory provided, while Chloe just gave him a shocked look, "is Purple Princess's best friend." And then she smiled.

And for a moment, everything in the world seemed to slowly grind to a halt. She was looking at him as if everything would turn out okay. As if everything was normal. She was Chloe's mom. He was Chloe's dad.

It scared the bloody hell right out of him.

"Now." She held out her hand for Chloe. "Come sit down with me and Ryan for a minute. There's something important you need to know."

"He *is* your boyfriend," Chloe trumpeted. "I *knew* it!"

Mallory's cheeks went red again. "No, sweetheart. He's…he's not. But—" She shot him a quick look. Not exactly filled with apology or defiance, but definitely full of something. Determination maybe. "But Ryan *is* someone very special. And I don't want to wait another minute to tell you. You see he's, well, he's your father."

He waited for the shock. The explosion. The denial or horror.

But Chloe just blinked a little as she absorbed the news.

And then she smiled more brightly than ever, turning that wonder-filled gaze on him again. "I knew this was going to be the bestest birthday ever! Now we're never ever going to have to leave Weaver, right?"

Chapter Thirteen

"You have a patient waiting in room two." Nina's disembodied voice sounded through the intercom in Mallory's office and she jumped a little. "Last-minute appointment."

Mallory glanced at her watch. It was nearly quitting time and had been a very quiet Monday afternoon as far as patients went. As for Mallory's emotions, it had been anything but, and had been that way since Chloe had jumped to the conclusion that being Ryan's daughter meant staying in Weaver from now on.

Mallory hadn't had the heart to correct her assumption on her birthday, and hadn't had a good opportunity to do so since then.

Ryan had been noticeably quiet on the issue, too.

"Thank you, Nina." She slipped the pile of snapshots from the birthday party that she'd been studying back into the paper envelope and left it on her desk. Kathleen had taken most of the photographs, and when Ryan had driven Mallory and Chloe to Braden yesterday to find a bed and a collar truly worthy of Abercrombie, they'd dropped the film off at a one-hour developer.

No digital cameras for Kathleen.

She preferred the old-fashioned method.

Whichever her preference, she'd managed to catch a lot of images. Not just from the party, but from the day that Chloe and Ryan had made the snowman.

So many of them with Chloe and Ryan. Chloe and Ryan and Mallory.

It was as if Kathleen had been determined to portray them as the family that they were. And weren't.

And Mallory knew that if she'd *really* wanted to disabuse Chloe of her notion that they were going to stay in Weaver now, she would have found time. Either during that day trip to Braden. Or before Chloe's bedtime last night. Or in the morning before she'd dropped her off at school.

She let out a sigh and slipped her stethoscope around the collar of her sweater as she went down the hall to the examining room. She pulled the chart from the pocket on the wall beside the door and the name on it jumped out at her.

Courtney Clay.

Frowning a little, Mallory glanced through the chart and, after knocking softly on the door, she went inside. Courtney was sitting on the exam table, paging through a magazine. She was fully dressed in a pair of pale blue scrubs.

Mallory shut the door softly. "You don't *look* like you're here for a routine exam," she said calmly, which was the reason Nina had listed. "Which makes sense since your chart here shows that Dr. Yarnell gave you a physical less than half a year ago." She set the chart on the counter and sat down on the round, rolling stool. "Are you all right? Do you have some health problem you didn't want to tell Nina about?" Ryan's sister certainly wouldn't have been the first patient to come in on some pretext, though Courtney was the first nurse Mallory had ever experienced doing so.

Courtney folded the magazine and set it on the chair next

to the examining table. "I want to know what you're doing with my brother."

Mallory inhaled, letting the statement settle while her thoughts whirled. She rolled her pen between her palms and wondered how Ryan would want her to answer, how much Courtney actually knew. They'd told Chloe the truth just two days ago, and the only other people to know were Kathleen, and Ryan's parents.

Other than physically giving Mallory a wide berth ever since the mistletoe business—and what had come before— he'd made no mention that he'd intended to share the news with anyone else, yet. Since she'd already introduced enough into his life by bringing Chloe to Weaver in the first place, she'd figured it should be his business how he chose to proceed with his own family.

Even though she'd been sleepless with a raging need to know. Not just because of Chloe, but because of *him*.

If she could just figure out what it was that he made her feel, she'd be much better able to deal with it. Instead, she felt constantly on edge.

She looked at his sister now. Courtney and Ryan had such different coloring, but there was definitely a similarity in the straight, fine line of their noses, the sweep of their brows.

Traits that Chloe shared.

"What has Ryan said?"

Courtney's eyes were shadowed. "If he'd said anything to me, do you think I'd resort to this?" Her long fingers lifted, encompassing the small examining room. "Ryan barely talks to me anymore, Dr. Keegan. Not since he… came back. I don't even know why. But obviously, he's involved with you, so if I have to find out from you what's going on, then I will."

There was such pained confusion in Courtney's face that

Mallory's heart hurt for her. She set aside her pen. This wasn't a doctor-patient moment. "This is really something you should work out with him."

"He was always pulling me out of one scrape or another. Ready to blow this pop stand, he'd ask me, and then he'd take me home. He even saved my life once." She pulled up one of the short sleeves covering her shoulder to reveal part of a faded scar that continued beneath the fabric. "I was twelve years old and playing in the park in town on the swing set. Swinging high and jumping off?"

Mallory nodded.

"Anyway, I swung too high and got tangled in the chains on the way down. I was unconscious when he found me. I woke up in the hospital and he was right there with me. Ready to blow this pop stand?" Her voice cracked and she blinked hard, smoothing down her sleeve. "I wasn't even supposed to be at the park. My father was on duty and my mother was at the hospital and I was supposed to be walking home from school. But I'd stopped off at the park. Ryan was home on leave from the navy. I wasn't even a half hour late and he went looking for me."

"Good thing," Mallory breathed. It was no wonder Ryan had overreacted when Chloe had broken her arm.

"He was always my hero. I was devastated when he went missing. We finally had a memorial service for him." Her eyes met Mallory's. "And then last winter, he walks back into our lives on the night Axel and Tara got married. It was a miracle. I can live with the fact that he's changed. Because he's back and he's alive and that's the bottom line. Since he's started seeing you, he's *looked* alive. Okay. Happy. I heard he's even moved out of that damn motel and into a *house* right by you." She glanced around the examining room. "I just want to know that he's going to stay that way."

"Courtney—"

"I know you're not here to stay. So what happens to my brother when you go, Dr. Keegan?"

She sighed a little, dismayed. "I understand your concern."

"Do you?" Courtney's chin gained a stubborn angle that was distinctly like her brother's. "Have *you* lost a brother?"

"I lost my mother when I was fifteen," she countered softly. Gently. "And my sister seven years ago. And there's no possibility that either can come back."

Courtney's impossibly beautiful face fell. "God. I'm sorry."

Mallory covered Courtney's hand with her own. "You don't have anything to be sorry about. You're Ryan's sister. You know him far better than I do. Give him time." Look how far he'd come in just the few weeks since he'd learned about Chloe. The man was full of caring, if only he allowed himself to show it. And she wished she could tell Courtney that, if only to point out what was possible.

Courtney's hand turned in hers, though, squeezing with obvious urgency. "Do you care about him?"

Mallory's lips parted but the words caught in her throat. Yes, she cared about him. He was her daughter's father.

He's more than that.

She mentally batted at the whispering thought. "It's more complicated than that, Courtney."

"Why? Because he's Chloe's father?"

She started with surprise. "He did tell you, then."

"Not likely." Courtney let go of Mallory's hand and slid off the examining table to pace the close confines of the room. "Everyone in town is talking about it."

Mallory nearly choked. "How? Why? We haven't told anyone."

At that, Courtney almost looked amused. And a little pitying. "You really aren't used to living in a small town, are you. Gossip, Dr. Keegan, is Weaver's largest industry. If my mother hadn't called me this morning to clue me in to what y'all have been hiding, then I would have gotten to hear the news from Bonnie Tanner. She was busy serving it up this morning in the hospital cafeteria, along with the oatmeal."

"Tanner. Jenny Tanner was at Chloe's birthday party."

"She's Bonnie's daughter."

Mallory exhaled. Of course. Mallory hadn't been talking about their personal business with anyone else. Ryan hadn't been, either.

But Chloe?

"I'm sorry," she said quietly.

"For what? Obviously Chloe's the reason you came to Weaver."

"And she's responsible for the change you've noticed in your brother. It has nothing to do with me."

"I think you're wrong about that. So I'm just asking you to, well, to be careful." Her expression was serious. "He'd want to strangle me if he knew I was talking to you like this."

Mallory could well imagine. "You're trying to watch out for your big brother," she said. And that was something she also understood. She'd tried watching out for Cassie.

"Yes." Courtney looked awkward for a moment. "Well. Anyway, I should let you get back to your real work. I just didn't want anyone overhearing us, and this was the only place I could think of."

"The examining room is out of bounds for gossip?"

"Yeah." She slipped her gleaming hair behind her ear and plucked her coat off the hook on the wall. "I suppose you'll all be at the Christmas festival on Saturday?"

It would have been nice to say that she'd barely given the matter any thought, but it would have been a lie. Both Chloe and Kathleen had talked about the town's holiday event. As had every one of the patients that Mallory had seen almost since she'd arrived in town. "I haven't made plans to," she said honestly.

"The whole family will be there. Seems right that you guys be there, too."

Mallory really didn't imagine that Ryan would voluntarily put himself in that setting, but she kept the thought to herself. The man was full of surprises, after all.

So, really, what did she know?

"We'll see." She picked up the medical file and walked with Courtney out to the reception area. "Are you off for the day?"

Courtney shook her head. "Haven't been in yet. I'm on from five to five."

"Long night shift."

"It's not so bad. It's usually pretty quiet. Thanks again." Courtney smiled at Nina and headed toward the door.

Mallory wasn't certain what she'd done to earn any thanks, but she watched until the younger woman had gone out the door. Then she looked at Nina. It was straight up four o'clock and the woman was already wielding her keys over the filing cabinets, locking everything up tight. "Are you going to the Christmas festival, Nina?"

The other woman's shoulders looked rigid. "I don't have a date." Her voice was tight.

"I thought it was more of a family kind of thing."

Nina looked over her shoulder. "Ending with a dinner-dance," she said as if any dunce should know. "A woman doesn't go to that sort of thing without a date."

Mallory stifled the urge to ask Nina what century she was living in. "What about going with your girlfriends?" She wouldn't hazard a guess to Nina's age, but figured she probably had ten years or so on Mallory. "Couldn't you go with a group and not worry about a date at all? That's what I used to do back home." On those rare occasions that she'd not been working and had actually done something that didn't involve Chloe.

Which only made Mallory think back to how long ago that had been.

"Why do *you* care?" Nina's voice was so particularly waspish that Mallory felt the sting.

"I really don't know," she snapped back, only to regret it as soon as she did. "Nina, I don't know what I've done to upset you, but we've got to work together for a while yet and—"

"That's right," Nina interrupted. She yanked her purse out of the bottom drawer of her desk and slammed it shut. "As if I need any sort of reminder from you that Dan needed to get away from his life here so badly he had to go to Asia! If you hadn't come here, he would never have left."

She flew out the door so fast that Mallory barely had a chance to absorb what she'd said. But the door opened again barely a second later. "Nina—"

It was Ryan who entered, though, and her mouth went dry at the sight of him.

"You always have women racing out of your office like that?"

Even though they hadn't discussed any specific plans, she half expected to see Chloe on his heels. But the door softly swung shut after his entrance and there was definitely no Chloe. "That was Nina," she said absently. "I think I finally know what her problem with me is. Where's Chloe?"

"With your grandmother and Abercrombie." He unzipped his jacket, surveying the interior. "I went by your place after I finished up out at J.D.'s place, but they banished me from the house."

Somehow, she didn't think he'd come straight from his cousin's place. She'd only seen him in T-shirts or sweaters and jeans, but today he had on an ivory button-down shirt that looked suspiciously like silk tucked into the waist of very finely tailored charcoal trousers. Hardly the kind of clothing to wear working around a barn and horses.

"Christmas gifts," Mallory deduced, trying not to give in to her raging curiosity or the desire to stand there and drool a while. *Why* did the man have to look so good?

"Not for me, I hope."

She let out a laugh. "Why not for you? Who else would they be for if they didn't want you around?"

He shoved his hand through his hair, looking distinctly disconcerted and she was ashamed to take more than a little pleasure in it since so often *she* was the one who felt off-kilter.

"Don't worry." She forgot to wonder what he was doing at her office in the first place in favor of taking pity on him. "It's probably something handmade and edible. Lemon bread. Cookies." She moved across the reception area to lock the door.

He looked slightly relieved. "I guess that's okay, then."

She bit back a smile and walked around Nina's desk to switch the phone lines over to the answering service.

"Courtney was here?"

She looked up to see Ryan staring down at the clearly labeled file still sitting on the desk. She picked it up and put it into Nina's desk drawer since the filing cabinets were already locked. "She came by."

His brows twitched together and he followed her up the hallway as she made her way to the rear of the office, shutting off lights as she went. "What for?"

"Ryan, she's a patient here." She shook her head a little. "What do you expect me to tell you?"

"Is she sick? *Pregnant?*"

"For heaven's sake!" She turned on him, her hands on her hips. "Even if she were—and I'm not saying anything of the sort—I could not discuss it with you without her permission even if she is your sister."

He certainly had to understand that particular point, but instead, he simply looked adamant. "I have a right to know if she's all right."

She exhaled. It wasn't the first time she'd encountered such an attitude from a concerned father or husband, but it was certainly unexpected coming from Ryan. "She's not all right," she returned, lifting her hand to ward off any jumping to conclusions he seemed ready to make. "But only because she's concerned about *you*."

She could almost catalog the shutting down of emotion on his face. The tightening of his lips. The smoothing of his forehead. The flattening of his sapphire gaze. "She shouldn't waste time worrying about me."

"Just because you happen to hold that opinion doesn't mean anyone else does." She walked into the small break room that was little more than a closet. She shut off the coffeemaker that sat on top of the narrow, short refrigerator and turned off the light. She had to pass within inches of Ryan to do so, and her nerves jangled foolishly. They hadn't been alone together since Saturday morning in his house, and what had transpired there was dangerously fresh in her mind. "Courtney certainly doesn't share it."

"She came here to talk to *you* about me?"

She was beginning to wish she'd simply maintained her silence about the entire matter. Ryan already knew what sort of strain existed between him and his sister. He was also the only one who knew the reason for it and he wasn't sharing with Mallory any more than he was sharing with Courtney.

She headed into Dan's office since there was nothing left around the place to lock up or shut down. "She asked if we'd be at the festival this weekend." It was hardly all that Courtney had said, but at least divulging this much didn't feel like breaking a confidence. "Evidently the news about Chloe is making the rounds. Chloe told one of the girls in her class that you were her father and it's—" she waved her hand expressively "—apparently gone from there. Your mom told Courtney before someone else could." Since *he* hadn't.

"Why would Chloe tell some other kid?"

"Why wouldn't she? Or didn't you happen to notice that she was more than a little excited over learning that particular fact?" Excited. Delighted. Even more so over Ryan than she had been about Abercrombie. Which was saying something. "She's happy to learn that you're her father, and she wants to talk about it with her friends. Obviously." And Mallory felt ridiculous for not having foreseen and prevented this very thing.

She sat down behind the desk and toyed with the thick envelope of Kathleen's snapshots. Ryan had a set, too, courtesy of the free double prints, and she knew he'd looked through them, because they'd done it while sitting in the close confines of his truck cab outside the photo shop.

She'd wondered then if he'd seen the same thing in them as she had.

What *looked* like a family.

Her eyes tracked his movements as he paced from one side of the office to the other, stopping now and then to pick up a picture or a book from the collection on the bookshelves that Dan had left and Mallory hadn't disturbed.

He was obviously restless and not making any attempt to hide it.

Which in turn made her distinctly nervous. "Did you come here to talk about Chloe?"

He finally stopped pacing and pulled an envelope from the inside of his jacket. "In a matter of speaking. Here." He dropped the envelope on the desk in front of her.

She drew her fingers away from it. "What's that?"

"It's an envelope." His voice was dry. "And it's not going to bite. So just open it already."

She wished he couldn't read her thoughts so easily. "Don't be so impatient."

He made a soft sound. "Some things just happen naturally when I'm around you."

She felt abruptly scorched and her gaze flew up to his, which did not improve the situation. A lump lodged in her throat and she hastily lowered her lashes, looking at the envelope again.

Suddenly, it seemed far less dangerous to focus on it rather than getting caught up in the blue fire of his eyes. She tore open the envelope and extracted the folded papers inside. As she did so, a bank check slid out from the center.

She frowned a little, glancing at it, only to do a double take at the number of zeros scrawled in his slanting black script. She dropped the check on the desk and shoved back in her wheeled chair so hard that it rocked against the credenza behind her. "Is this some sort of joke?"

He moved the check from the edge of the desk back to the center of the leather blotter. "I've never thought that much money was all that funny."

She looked from his face back to the check. It was an astronomical sum, with his name imprinted on one corner, his signature on the other. Her name stood out clearly in the center of it all. "You can't have money like this."

But his perfectly serious expression told her that he most certainly could.

"Maybe I should have gone to handyman school," she quipped, but the humor fell flat. "I'm probably going to regret this, but what on earth did you do to earn that kind of money?"

"What if I told you I inherited it?"

She watched him narrowly. It was possible, she supposed. Since living in Weaver, she'd learned that the Clay family in general were quite well-off, mostly because of the Double-C Ranch. It was unusually large. And uncommonly successful. But his father was the retired sheriff and, while his mother was the administrator at the hospital, Mallory doubted that even Rebecca earned half of what the check was worth.

Something in Ryan's expression told her this wasn't related in any way to that, anyway. "I'd say you weren't telling me the truth. And I'm quite certain you didn't earn it in the navy, or every red-blooded boy and girl in this country would have enlisted by now. So…?" She lifted her eyebrows, waiting.

"HW Industries paid well."

She snorted. "Not that well. Cassie had a healthy nest egg saved up, but it was gone in the first year, primarily thanks to Chloe's medical expenses."

"What's *that* supposed to mean?" His hands were suddenly planted on the desk in front of her as he leaned closer. "Chloe was sick?"

"She was premature," Mallory reminded him. "She had some heart issues that required surgery. And now she's perfectly fine. But even with insurance, that sort of care comes with a price tag and I was grateful to have Cassie's savings to fall back on." Particularly when she, herself, had been nearly incapable of working for months after her sister's death.

She picked up the check and waved it between them. "And distracting me isn't going to work, Ryan. What is all of this about?"

"It would just be easier if you'd read the papers," he said gruffly.

Easier maybe, but she was painfully afraid to do so. Particularly in light of the check.

She'd legally adopted her niece. But Ryan was Chloe's natural father and, evidently, a very wealthy one at that.

If he were to force the issue of Chloe's custody, what sort of chance would she stand against him?

She finally exhaled and snatched up the papers, unfolding them with fingers that visibly trembled. But instead of custody papers, or even child-support issues, it was a will.

Ryan's will.

And in it, he was leaving all of his worldly possessions to his daughter, Chloe Kathleen Keegan. And naming Mallory as the trustee until Chloe reached her majority.

Her chest grew tight. Achy. She flipped past the concise

will to the second page. It was a bank statement of some sort, but not like any that she'd ever seen. "I don't understand."

"That's a trust for you and Chloe. You can use it however you see fit. Chloe's education. Housing for the three of you. Medical. Pay off your school loans if you want. It's all set up for you. You just have to go into the bank sometime soon to sign a paper or two."

A paper or two. She felt as if she'd dropped down the rabbit hole. Her eyes finally found the bottom line of the statement and the amount there made the check seem nearly minor in comparison.

Ryan wasn't wealthy. He was rich. Period.

"What if I wanted to go live in Tahiti," she asked faintly. "Donate hundreds of thousands to further research in ant migration?"

He smiled faintly. "You wouldn't."

"How do you know that!"

"Because you're my daughter's mother and everything you do is because of her. And because I trust you."

Chapter Fourteen

Mallory's eyes suddenly burned. She carefully refolded the papers and placed them, along with the check, back inside the envelope. And that she set carefully in the center of the desk blotter, where it sat staring up at her like a rectangular, white eye.

The only sound in the building came from the soft gurgling of the filter on the aquarium.

She finally looked up at him. "What do you expect in exchange for all of this?"

His eyes narrowed. "Exchange?"

"Yes. Exchange." Nervous energy propelled her out of her chair, but that only succeeded in leaving her nowhere to move except to the other side of the desk where *he* was. It was either that, or sit back down, and she badly needed to be on her feet. It gave her some sense of equality with him, even if it was only an illusion. "My agreement that I won't take Chloe back with me to New York, I suppose?"

He let out a rough breath. "I'm not trying to buy Chloe, Mallory. I'm not trying to take her away from you at all. Christ, if that's what I'd wanted, I'd be in here with my attorney!"

She folded her arms across her chest, feeling she was sinking deeper into a hole that was lined with questions she had no hope of getting answered. "Then what *do* you want?"

"The impossible." He turned away from her and moved to the window that overlooked the street and the empty antique store across the way. The light outside was already slanting toward evening. "I want my life to be what it used to be, and it's never going to happen."

She fiddled with the stethoscope that she'd forgotten around her neck. "Because of Chloe?"

"Because of me." He turned to look at her. But his face was in shadow and all she could hear was that flat, emotionless tone of voice that tore at her insides. "Because of the things I've done that I can't undo."

She could barely draw a breath for fear that he wouldn't continue. For fear that he would. And that whatever wounds he carried inside him were far beyond her ability to heal. "What things?"

"You really want to know how I came by the money?"

Did she? What if he'd been involved in something illegal. Something unsavory and—

She shut off the ridiculous thoughts.

He wasn't just anyone.

He was Ryan. Cassie had trusted him.

And even if not for Cassie, *Mallory* knew in her heart that she trusted him, too. If she hadn't, she never would have told Chloe that he was her father.

"Yes," she said softly. "I want to know."

"I helped buy and sell beautiful girls just like my sister to the highest bidder. Ten years old. Twelve. Fifteen. Didn't matter, just as long as they were blonde and ivory-skinned and full of innocence."

Her heart seemed to stop beating for what seemed an eternity. She couldn't see his expression, but she could see the way his hands were rolled into fists.

Before she even realized she'd done it, she took a step toward him. "I don't believe you."

"Why? Because you think I wouldn't admit it if it were true?" A jetliner could have landed in the void of his voice.

She took another step.

He was stuck between the desk, the window…and her.

"Because you're not capable of doing any such thing."

"Well, believe it, Doc. I worked right alongside a man who's a brother to the devil himself and I couldn't stop him. So if you were smart—and we both know you are—you'd take that money and run."

With every minute that passed, the sky outside the window was turning darker. But a light inside her head was starting to glimmer.

The money wasn't an attempt to make her stay.

It was a reason to get her to go.

"*That's* what all that—" she waved toward the desk "—is about, isn't it? It's just a tool for you. Some method of trying to convince me you're not fit to be a father."

"Are you listening to a word I've said?"

"I'll listen when the words you say are the truth! The whole truth and not some…some piece of whatever horror it is that you're carrying around with you!" She was shaking inside, but she wasn't going to let that stop her. She wasn't going to be silent now, when someone mattered this much.

Someone?

Ryan.

She stopped directly in front of him. "What are you afraid of? Chloe already has you wrapped around her finger. You already care." He hadn't been able to hide that. Who could when one was dealing with Chloe's generous heart? "The worst has happened, so why try to get us out of the picture now?" Lord knows they were going to have to go soon enough.

He'd seemed fine when they'd driven to Braden and traipsed through stores and eaten lunch at a hole-in-the-wall deli and driven home again with Chloe falling asleep on the seat between them.

What had happened since then to make him take such action?

"Right now I'm a novelty to Chloe. She was fine before she knew about me and she'll be fine after, too."

His choice of words sent a tidal wave of dismay coursing through her. "You make it sound as if you've already decided to disappear from her life!"

His fists became hands again, his fingers latching onto her shoulders with obvious restraint as he nudged her aside until she was no longer blocking his exit.

Then he let her go as if he couldn't bear to touch her.

"I'm not going to take this money, Ryan," she said to his back as he started to leave the office. "Not a dime of it."

He stopped and pivoted on his heel to face her again. "Dammit, Mallory. At least be smart about this."

"This is probably the smartest thing I've ever done," she said swiftly. "You think that money—the way you claim you earned it, I guess—gives you an exit pass from your daughter's life and you are wrong!"

"You've got a name for that empty baby book page, and now you've got enough money to give her everything she'll need to grow up and be like you."

"And *not* like you? That's what you really mean, isn't it?"

"I'm not the kind of man you should want for your daughter."

"What would you like me to do, then, Ryan?" She spread her hands. "Go find some nice, suitable man to marry and *he* can be the one to help Chloe with her homework and teach her to drive and scare off her first boyfriend and walk her down the aisle when she gets married? Is that what you want?"

He slammed his knuckles against the bookcase and she jumped.

But his voice, when it finally came, held no violence. "No," he said. His voice was simply…defeated.

And just that quickly, she wanted to weep.

And it had nothing whatsoever to do with their daughter. Her heart would be breaking for him if there were no Chloe at all.

But there was, or they wouldn't be here right now at all.

As if he no longer possessed the energy to stand, he sank down on the edge of the desk. He ran his palm down his face. "No," he said again.

Quaking inside, she stepped up to him, slowly lifted her hand and stroked back the thick hair above his temple. She kissed his forehead as gently as she kissed Chloe when she didn't want to wake her. "It will be all right," she whispered.

He closed his eyes. A soundless sigh worked through him.

And then his hands slid around her waist and he pulled her into his body. His head found her shoulder.

She wrapped her arms around him. Pressed her cheek to his head. If there was nothing else she could accomplish, she was desperate to give him some ease.

So she stood there.

Just holding him while her heart ached and his arms held her so tightly she could feel the anguish writhing inside him like some tangible beast. Just holding him as the light outside the windows slanted even more deeply into shadow and the office grew dimmer and the light inside the aquarium on the credenza grew brighter, casting a small, warm glow.

She didn't know exactly when the tension inside them both shifted, but it did. And his palms were flat against her spine, the warmth of his breath drifting over her neck, the faint rasp of his jaw abrading the underside of her chin.

And when his mouth found hers, she was waiting.

As if she'd been waiting her entire life.

There was no playing around, no teasing, no tempting. Just an endless, consuming, deep kiss from which she never wanted to surface.

But a person has to breathe and, eventually, necessity simply won out.

Her head fell back as she hauled in oxygen, feeling his chest expand against her while he did the same. Through her sweater she could feel the imprint of every one of his fingers against her back and craved the feel of them on her skin, instead.

"We're going to make love on this desk unless there's another spot in this office." His voice was low. Rough. And it sent a thrilling ripple through the very core of her.

"Couch." She managed to form the words. "In the reception area."

He pushed off the desk and his hands moved to her hips, tightening dangerously there for a long, long moment as he held her fast.

She felt branded by him. And sucked in a startled breath when he suddenly moved and lifted her up. One of her black leather pumps slipped right off her foot, but she barely noticed as his mouth covered hers again, stealing every speck of caution that still remained.

She was vaguely aware of motion; he was carrying her out of the office. Down the darkened hall. Unerringly ending in the reception area where he followed her down onto the couch that had been designed more to accommodate as many patients as possible than for comfort.

With one strong arm beneath her, he positioned her along the narrow length, and settled between her thighs.

They were still both fully clothed, but her fingers

greedily gathered that nubby silk fabric, tugging it free of his belt until she could reach the hot skin beneath. And he was no less impatient, his fingertips grazing against her as he undid the tiny pearl-like buttons of her peach-colored sweater. And when he reached the hem, he smoothed it to the sides as if he were unwrapping a precious gift. Then slowly, so slowly she could have cried, he pressed his mouth to the hollow of her throat and moved his hands beneath the thin knit to close over her breasts, and she nearly bowed off the couch altogether.

He made a soft, wordless sound. Male. Approving. So deeply erotic that she felt buffeted by need.

He found the center clasp of her bra and stripped the thin cups away and then his thumbs were brushing over and around her anxiously tight nipples. She fisted her hands in his hair, dragging his mouth back to hers.

He made that low sound again and kissed her. Hotter. Harder. She moaned with frustration when he slipped away again before she was at all satisfied.

He pushed off the couch, but her protest died when she heard the jangle of his belt buckle. The rustle of clothing. In the dark, she could only make out the tall, broad shape of him, the faint sheen of flesh as he moved.

And then his hands were on her waist again. Unerringly finding the zipper of her slacks, drawing it down, stripping away her clothes with such certain, purposeful movements that she felt dizzy. And then there was nothing at all between them.

Not even a breath.

Her legs slid against his, reveling in the rougher texture, the roping shape and length of his calves, the bunching of his thighs when her fingers trailed from the crisp whorls of hair on his chest and down his ribs to his hips. "We should have turned on the light," she whispered only to end on a groan when she felt his mouth close over her nipple. "I want to see you."

"You won't like what you see."

"I doubt that." Her hands followed the slope of his back. Dipped lower over hard, tight curves and tried to pull him even closer, to end the torment and take everything that she was so desperately willing to give. "You're killing me."

"Now you know how I feel. Nearly every time I close my eyes, this is what's in my head." He slowly moved over her until his mouth was brushing against hers. Her breasts were crushed beneath the hard wall of chest. His hands caressed her thighs. Shaped her knees. Climbed again, only this time on the inside.

Her head fell back and she cried out when his hand found the center of her. Eager. Wet. Ready. "Please—" He was pushing too fast, too hard, and she was going to come apart at the seams. And she wanted him to be a part of her, first. She twined her legs around his. "Ryan, I can't wait—"

"I can't either." With one stroke, he claimed her.

She gasped, the pleasure careening through her reaching a mindless pitch.

His hands found hers, fingers threading, palms meeting. She could hear his harsh breath and feel his racing heart, which matched her own.

This wasn't just sex. Basic lovemaking.

It was a total and complete undoing of her sense of self.

She didn't know where either one of them began or ended.

Nor did it matter, as the whirlwind tightened, binding them together in a hungry, spinning frenzy before it catapulted them into perfection.

And when he groaned her name and his arms tightened around her like iron bands that might never set her free, Mallory knew that there was one place in the universe for her to be, and this was it.

In Ryan's arms.

* * *

"Something's poking me in the hip," she said a long while later.

The world had stopped spinning. Their hearts had stopped racing.

But she knew she would never be the same.

His soft laughter was rippling through her. "No kidding."

She weakly batted his shoulder. "I'm serious." She wriggled around, trying to reach the small, hard ridge digging into her.

"You're going to give me a heart attack if you keep wiggling like that," he complained, sounding so lazily satisfied that she couldn't help but smile into the dark.

Holding her against his chest, he rolled even more to the side—somehow managing not to land them both on the floor—and swept his hand between her and the back of the couch.

He found the object and pulled it out. "Somebody's been playing doctor."

She could see the shadowy outline of her stethoscope. "So it would seem."

He kept shifting until she found herself suddenly sprawled on top of him.

"When I was a kid, my mother was very strict about letting me mess with her doctor stuff."

"Is that a technical term?" Mallory smiled faintly. "And being strict is sometimes what mothers do."

He put the earpieces to his ears and then placed the chest piece against her chest. His wrist brushed against her sensitized nipple.

Deliberately, she suspected, and didn't have a single protest to make.

"Your heartbeat sounds very fast," he observed with undue seriousness.

"That's what *you* do," she said softly. It seemed fantastical that she could still want more of him when her body ached tenderly in places where it hadn't for years; when she didn't seem to have left a solid bone or muscle, but she did.

She tugged the stethoscope away from him and started to slide off him, but his arms held her in place and, even though she knew they couldn't remain there indefinitely, she willingly subsided.

Her head found the curve between his strong neck and shoulder, and her hand settled on his wide, deep chest.

She didn't need her stethoscope to hear his rhythmic pulse. It was almost lulling enough to put her to sleep.

Except that his fingers kept drifting slowly up and down her spine, and the shivers that danced through her were anything but lulling.

"I think Nina had something going with Dr. Yarnell," she murmured after a moment.

He gave a faint laugh. "You're officially a Weaver resident now, Doc. I think that was gossip."

"Maybe so." The idea of being more than a temporary resident had never had more appeal than it did now. But she was also very aware that he'd never suggested that she consider making their stay in Weaver a permanent one.

And her career was waiting for her back in New York.

Which was something that she simply didn't want to think about just then.

So she rubbed her foot along his calf, instead.

She touched the tip of her tongue to the curve of his neck. Salty. Addictive.

"I'm not kidding about the heart attack," he grumbled softly.

"Oh?" Her voice was innocent, but the hand she slipped boldly between them to wrap around him was not.

She felt him drag air into his lungs. "Doc—"

Grumbling or not, he was hard.

And she was so…not.

She rose over him, taking the very tip of him into her tender body. She held still, letting the urgency to take more settle and calm until it was a low, insistent beating in her veins. "Is there a problem?" Her muscles intimately flexed and he gave a strangled sound.

Ryan's fingers tightened around her hips while he fought the urge to flip Mallory onto her back and bury himself in her as deeply as he'd just done. "What does it feel like to you?"

She dipped her hips infinitesimally, but it was still enough to make his jaw go tight and his control slip dangerously near the edge of his grasp.

"It feels…perfect."

He hoped to hell she was causing herself no small amount of torment.

"*You* feel perfect," she added, and did that little dip thing again. He swore he saw white behind his eyes.

Not red as in passion. Not red as in hell.

White.

As in heaven, which was what it felt like inside of her.

And it felt like all the rules were changing, sliding right out of his grasp. The tighter he tried to hold on, the slipperier they became.

He'd realized it under the mistletoe. And during Chloe's birthday party when they were surrounded by a half-dozen chattering little girls and he hadn't wanted to escape, just because Mallory was in the room, her amber eyes warm and her beautiful mouth smiling. And then when it was just the three of them, hunting down dog gear in Braden.

He hadn't wanted to run.

He hadn't wanted to do anything but stay with them.

And where would that get any of them?

So he'd visited the bank and taken care of the trust. He'd called up his cousin-in-law, Brody Paine, who was an attorney. He'd told Ryan what needed to be said in the will. And then if that wasn't enough, he had written that check.

And then he'd slapped it all down in front of Mallory,

knowing that she'd want an explanation, and once she had it, he wouldn't have to run.

Because she would do it for him.

Only she hadn't believed him.

And she hadn't run.

And now, all he could do was hang on while she took him inside her body with such aching slowness that his eyes burned deep inside his head.

She set her palm in the center of his chest, right above the spot where his rusty heart was chugging, and leaned over him until her mouth hovered above his. "Where are you going, Ryan?" Her voice was soft. Beckoning. She brushed her lips against his. "Come back to me."

The burning got worse. So he just tightened his hands around the perfect flare of her hips and thrust into her.

He heard her inhale. Felt her fingertips flex, pressing hard into his chest.

And then she was moving again and those soft, breathy sounds were rising in her throat. He closed his eyes and let the world...go...white.

Chapter Fifteen

"I'm sorry I didn't get you called earlier, Gram. I've been at the office." Mallory's gaze met his across Nina's desk where she was using the phone. "I had a…a late appointment come in."

Even across the room, he could see the flush that hit her cheeks at that and, as if she knew it, she turned her head, until she wasn't looking at him at all. It just gave him a good view of her slender back, perfectly illuminated by the light that she'd turned on before making her call.

"You and Chloe have already eaten dinner, right?" She tucked the phone in the crook of her neck and pulled her slacks up over her long, lovely legs.

The vision of her dressing would be branded in his brain forever. He finally looked away to finish pulling on his own clothes. With each layer he put on, the peace he'd found in the past few hours seemed less and less real.

He realized she'd finished her call when she padded over to him and plucked her bra off the corner of the coffee table littered with out-of-date magazines. She turned away while she quickly fastened the bra as if she'd been struck by a bolt of shyness. "Chloe had a good day and is already getting ready for bed," she reported.

But he caught the falseness beneath the chipper tone and that peace slipped a little more toward unreality.

He picked up the rest of the clothes—his shirt, her sweater. "Here."

"Thanks." She slipped her arms into the sweater only to stop and catch his hand. "Look at your knuckles!"

He flexed them. "Nothing's broken." They were red. Some were split but the thin bloody lines were dried.

She huffed anyway. "Small wonder when you go around punching mahogany shelves." She pulled him with her down the hallway and into the first examining room. "Sit."

Her voice brooked no argument, and he sat. But he eyed the metal stirrups that were folded out of the way at the end of the padded table. "Could have been interesting in here," he murmured, mostly to get a reaction.

"Only if *you're* the one in them," she returned with such aplomb that he was damned if his own neck didn't get hot.

He caught her faint smile as, much to his regret, she finished buttoning her sweater before rummaging through the drawers under the counter. She dropped a few packets on the table beside him and tore one open, swabbing over the cut.

"Jesus, Doc." He yanked his hand away at the fierce sting. "Pour some acid on it while you're at it."

She gave him a straight look that did nothing whatsoever to hide her amusement and held out her hand, waiting for him to put his paw back.

Which he did, feeling about as manly as a mouse.

She dabbed again and, though it stung like a mother, he managed not to squeal again. And in quick order, she'd wrapped and taped up his knuckles. "Would you like a sucker?" Her voice was angelic, the smile tugging at the corners of her lips exactly the opposite.

"Kissing it works better."

She lifted his hand, her eyes never leaving his, and pressed her mouth softly to the gauze. "What about this one?" She trailed her other hand down the scar beneath his arm and he went still. "Who kissed that one better?"

He should have known she'd see it. It wasn't hard to miss the distinct scar among his ribs when the lights were on and his shirt was off.

He could have lied. Told her any story more palatable than the truth. But the truth was what it would take to make her realize that some things just didn't get better. "The hooker who found me in an alley in Kuala Lumpur."

"Pretty messy stitchery." She didn't look anywhere near as shocked as he figured she should.

"Yeah, well, I didn't have great pickings." The girl who'd found him had taken him to a friend of hers who'd stitched the gash with rudimentary and not exactly sterile skill. None of them had wanted to draw attention to themselves. Not from the law or from Krager's people.

Her palm covered the ugly scar and her light touch felt as if it might well burn right through his rib cage. "How did it happen?"

"I got knifed."

She just watched him with those soft, earnest eyes. And her voice was even softer. "What really happened with those girls, Ryan? What were you really doing? Who were they?"

"People's daughters. Sisters." The only times he didn't see their terrified faces when he closed his eyes was when he was seeing Mallory there, instead.

Heaven. Or hell.

"Snatched from wherever, whenever. Taken to one of the houses where we guarded them until the devil himself set up his next auction." He pinched the bridge of his nose. Krager just kept getting richer and cagier, and those poor girls had kept rolling in. Runaways. Kidnappings. Didn't matter as long as they'd fit the product description. And no matter how often Ryan had managed to leak the location of a house, the time and place of an auction, Krager had always slipped through. The most they'd ever netted were flunkies. Guys, just like he'd started out being, hoping to work their way up Krager's system to where the real power was.

"I wasted three years trying to earn the trust of the top lieutenants so I could get close enough to the guy in charge— Krager—and bring the whole network down, but it was never enough. Not even Krager's closest people knew the entire picture, so nobody could ever pin anything directly on him, because nobody ever could put together the entire puzzle. His network's unbelievable. Operates out of at least eight different countries. And those were just the ones we knew about."

"We?" Her voice was faint. She looked appalled.

"Hollins-Winword. HW Industries," he elaborated, feeling indescribably tired. "It's a private agency concerned with security. Domestic. International. You name it, they've had their fingers in it." And he'd been up to his neck. "They'll work with the government when they can, but a lot of what we did was off the map."

"*Cassie* was involved with this agency?" Her brows knitted. "She said she did business translating."

"She did. She wasn't in the field. Even companies like HW need admin and tech support. Cassie wasn't lying."

"But how did she ever get involved with them?"

He grimaced. "HW recruits specific people for specific skills from all over." His own family had turned into prime pickings. He supposed there were others, too.

"What was your skill?" she asked warily.

"Numbers. Patterns. The fact that I came from Naval Intelligence. Had a better than average proficiency with weapons." That was an understatement. And if he never held another gun he'd be happy.

"And this?" Her fingertip traced the jagged scar.

He looked down at his hands. "There was a girl, snatched from a school group. She could have been Courtney's twin," he said gruffly. "Tall. Stacked. Innocent as hell. I'd heard Krager was planning something special for her." Maybe it was the accumulation of years or the fact that she'd been a ringer for his kid sister or just the fact that he was losing his mind. But he'd snapped. "I didn't even know her real name. The guards called her Nadia. I tried to get her out. Same way I managed to get others out—smuggling them in piles of dirty laundry or whatever else was handy.

"But she didn't trust me any more than she trusted the other bastards guarding her and instead of saving her, I got myself stabbed and her drugged and dragged off all over again."

"Oh, Ryan." She had tears on cheeks.

"Don't cry for me." The words seemed to dredge up from somewhere deep in the earth. "Cry for the girls. Cry for Nadia. Because, after a few days, while I was lying in a cheap room on a cheap mattress stitched up but alive and no closer to shutting that bastard down, she threw herself off the side of a yacht owned by the twisted SOB who'd bought her. Her body was found by a local fisherman, otherwise it probably would've never even made the news. Nobody ever came forward to identify the body. I failed," he said roughly. In so many ways for too many years. "The things I've seen. Done. None of it's good, Mallory."

"You didn't always fail," she whispered. She took his face in her hands and rubbed her thumbs over his cheeks that he didn't even realize were as wet as hers. "What about the girls you helped get away?"

"I didn't help Nadia. I might as well have pushed her off that boat, myself. I blew cover, blew the entire op, and I didn't stick around to clean up the mess. I landed in Bangkok and tried to forget everything, including the people I'd left behind here."

"Another inch and you might not have lived long enough for that knife wound to even become a scar. You didn't push that poor girl. And you're back with your family now." She kept her gaze locked on his even when he wanted to look away. "Could you have done anything other than what you did? Was there some cavalry for you to call to the rescue?" She didn't flinch. "I can tell just by your face that there wasn't. You were the only cavalry they had, weren't you?"

"Don't try to make it heroic, Doc. Krager's still out there doing exactly what he's always done. And if not him, then someone else will take his place. And there will still be parents not knowing where to turn, brothers and sisters searching for someone they love and never finding them."

"All the more reason for you to connect with the family who is searching for *you,* right here! God, Ryan. You have people who love you all around you."

"They won't when they know what I've done."

"*I* know," she returned swiftly, "and I…" Her voice cut off but it was already too late.

The words floated in the air between them, spoken or not. *Love you.*

Fresh pain ripped down his chest. Hadn't he known better? "Don't confuse love with sex," he managed.

"I'm a doctor," she returned gently. "I'm quite certain I know the difference."

"You barely know me." Arguments, reason. They all started to gather steam.

"Do you know me?"

The steam evaporated. "What?"

"Who am I, Ryan? Other than Chloe's mom or the doctor who's filling in for Dan Yarnell for a few months. Do you *know* me?"

He wanted to say that he didn't. Or claim that he didn't know what the hell she was talking about.

But he couldn't look into those eyes and do it.

"You know what's in my head." She took his hand and pressed it to her breast. "You've seen what's in my heart."

What was in her heart was the kind of woman to raise a little girl who'd give a dollar to a complete stranger just because she thought he needed it more than she did. She was unselfish and compassionate. "Feeling sorry for me isn't love, either."

"Believe me," she said, her voice turning tart, "I don't pity you. You're stubborn and opinionated—"

"Like you are?"

"—and you never do what I expect—"

"Like you gave in on Abercrombie?"

"—and you helped me realize that it's okay to let Cassie go." She hesitated, probably waiting for him to counter that.

But he had nothing.

And the understanding in her eyes plainly told him that she'd known he wouldn't.

She ran her hands down his bare shoulders. Caught his hands between hers. "If you can help me finally start letting go of feeling responsible for Cassie's death, then how can you not do the same for yourself? Ryan, you were out there trying to make the world a better—a safer—place. For girls like your sister. Like your daughter. You said yourself, you helped some get away. Not every situation turned out like Nadia."

"Krager's still out there."

"Do *you* want to go out again to stop him, then?"

He'd already told Cole that he didn't. He shook his head.

"Maybe finding him isn't what you're meant to do."

He grimaced. "No kidding."

She squeezed his fingers. "Don't do that. Don't disparage

what you've already given. Sacrificed. You don't have to give up your own family to make up for not being able to do what nobody else has been able to do, either. If you want to help someone, help yourself first. And then maybe you can find some way to help those families who *don't* know where to turn. But please—" her voice lowered again, went husky "—please don't think that time—hours, days, weeks—can prevent me from seeing who you are. Not just here." She pressed her lips to his forehead. "But here." She pressed her palm against his heart.

"What if there comes a day when I can't protect Chloe?"

Mallory smiled shakily. "Welcome to parenthood."

The words seeped into him, still enough to make him shake in his boots. "I don't want to screw it up."

"None of us do. So you do the best that you can with what you've got. In Chloe's case, that's easy. Because who can *not* love her? She has a heart as wide as an ocean."

"She has *your* heart."

Her eyes went damp again. "I think she has more than a little of you as well. And Cassie."

This time it was Ryan who closed his hands around hers. They were so delicate. Yet Mallory was not.

She was strong and smart and independent and indescribably beautiful.

"So what do we do now, Doc?"

She inhaled. Let it out. "Now we go home and kiss your daughter good night before it gets any later."

It wasn't quite what he'd meant.

But for now, he realized, it was more than enough.

So he slid off the examining table, and she cleaned up the small mess from the antiseptic packets and bandages. When there was no sign whatsoever of all that had transpired in Dr. Yarnell's office, they went home.

* * *

"Mind if I cut in?"

Mallory glanced at the tall, spare man who'd tapped Ryan on the shoulder.

It was Saturday. The evening of the Christmas Festival dinner-dance and it was definitely not just an event for couples.

Even Nina must have come to terms with that, because Mallory had spotted the woman when they'd arrived, though Nina had pretended not to see *her*. Mallory also saw shy-faced men in boots and cowboy hats dancing with their little girls, and hospital nurses—including Courtney—getting their groove on the dance floor without a single male in sight. Though there were plenty of single ones eyeing them from where they hung out by the refreshment tables. The gymnasium had been decorated with miles of green garland and red ribbons. It wasn't at all fancy like some of the holiday parties she'd had to attend because of the practice in New York, but it was amazingly lovely.

And a whole lot more fun.

She'd danced with Ryan's father. His cousin Axel. His cousin-in-law, Evan, who'd looked amused when he'd asked how well the puppy was settling in. And even Jake Forrest, who was J. D. Clay's magazine-handsome fiancé, and one of Jake's decidedly precocious twin sons, though she still wasn't sure if it had been Connor or Zach.

And now, Ryan's grandfather, Squire Clay, was evidently prepared to interrupt the only dance she'd managed, so far, to actually share with *Ryan*.

"I don't mind as long as you swear you'll behave yourself," Ryan told the white-haired man.

Squire just smiled cannily with a glint in his sharp blue gaze and Mallory could instantly see where all of the Clay men had come by their good looks.

Ryan wasn't exactly the life of the party, but he was there and he was trying—he'd danced, once with his mother and once with Chloe—and now, the wry smile he sent Mallory was probably the most natural one she'd seen on his face since he'd walked in the gymnasium doors with her and Chloe and Kathleen. "Watch out for him," he warned Mallory. "He always flirts with the most beautiful women in the room."

Mallory couldn't help but glance over to the chaotic collection of round tables that had been shoved without ceremony closer together in one corner of the room to accommodate the mass of Ryan's family. Squire's wife, Gloria, was watching them, an indulgent, knowing smile on her still-lovely face. She was sitting next to Kathleen and throughout dinner the two women had talked of nothing but puppies and quilting and making predictions about whether the assortment of Clay women who were currently pregnant would be having a boy or a girl.

"Of course I pick the most beautiful women." Squire held out his arms. "Shall we?"

There was something irresistible about the man. And despite her very real interest in spending a little time in Ryan's arms since that particular treasure had been in short supply since that day in her office, she smiled and placed her hand in Squire's. "I'd be delighted, Mr. Clay."

"Child, I only answer to Squire or Grandpa, so take your pick." He was smiling as he swept her into an old-fashioned waltz that was disconcertingly graceful considering she'd seen him walking with a cane when they'd arrived. "That little Chloe of yours is a pip," he said after they'd swirled through the throng of dancers congesting the center of the gymnasium.

Mallory couldn't help feeling a tinge of wariness. Now that the news was out that Chloe was Ryan's daughter, everyone, whether family or not, had been unfailingly—if occasionally carefully—gracious. "She's certainly enjoying herself here," she offered. From the moment they'd arrived, Chloe had been a blur of motion in the purple-and-white-lace dress that

Kathleen had sewn for her. For every time Mallory had been on the dance floor, Chloe had been there twice.

No male was safe from her sights. Not little Ben Scalise who was only four, nor the Forrest twins who were a few years older than Chloe, and not even Ryan, himself. And then when she wasn't dancing, she was happily dividing her time among all of the laps of her newfound relations.

"My grandson is enjoying himself, too," Squire said. "We're mighty grateful to you for that."

Mallory shook her head. "Thank Chloe." Her daughter was the one who'd found the crack in Ryan's shell.

"Who wouldn't be here at all if not for you," he countered. "There aren't a lot of secrets that get kept for long in this family. I know it probably wasn't all that easy a decision to come here the way you did."

The decision to find Chloe's father had been a lot easier than what she faced now.

She had no illusions about her and Ryan. They would be forever linked because of Chloe. But just because she'd fallen in love with him didn't mean he felt the same. That he'd *ever* feel the same.

When it was time for her to take Chloe and Kathleen with her back to New York, she'd have to find a way to deal with it. It was one of those not-so-fine details that she had no clue how to resolve.

But that was months away. For now she fully intended to take what she could get.

"I don't regret it at all," she said now. "You have a wonderful family. I couldn't have wished for anything better for Chloe."

"And what about for you?"

She didn't know how to answer that. "I'm happy as long as Chloe is happy," she finally settled on.

There was something in the old man's eyes, though, that

told her he wasn't exactly convinced. But he said no more since the song was ending and the band announced that they were taking a break.

Mallory returned with Squire to the tables and he sat down next to his wife, closing his hand over hers with such clear devotion that she felt a little knot at the back of her throat. And as she glanced around, wondering where Ryan had gotten to, she realized that all of the couples at the tables seemed to exhibit that very same trait.

"I'm going to get some punch," she said to no one in particular. Chloe was now across the room along with a few dozen other children who were exploring the green-and-red wrapped packages that were stacked underneath the largest Christmas tree that Mallory had ever seen indoors. "Can I bring back anything?"

"I'll go, too." Rebecca stood up from her seat and the hem of her deep blue gown puddled a little on the floor since she'd kicked off her high heels without a speck of apology. Mallory envied her, but her own black dress was cocktail length and what Dr. Rebecca Clay could get away with wasn't necessarily the behavior that Mallory could.

"I've been wanting to talk with you, actually," Rebecca said when they were halfway toward the refreshments.

Mallory finally spotted Ryan, standing near the door talking with a white-haired man she didn't recognize. She focused with an effort on Ryan's mother. "About Chloe?"

They reached the punch table that had at least two dozen punch bowls, guarded by a pinched-faced woman to insure they didn't end up spiked. "About the hospital." Rebecca filled a plastic glass and handed it to Mallory.

"Hello, Dr. Clay." Nina stopped next to them to fill up her own glass. Her gaze barely grazed over Mallory. "Dr. Keegan."

"Nina. You look very nice tonight," Rebecca offered.

Nina swiped her hand down her long velvet skirt, obviously

self-conscious. "I came with friends." The look she slanted toward Mallory was almost defiant.

She wasn't going to take offense. Not when she was so certain now of the reason behind the other woman's animosity. "One of the best ways to enjoy a party. I'm glad to see you decided to come."

"Janie insisted she and Tom would stay home if I didn't come." She filled several glasses and picked them up carefully. "So here I am." Her smile was bright but there was a desperately sad edge to it as she turned away.

Mallory couldn't help feeling for the woman, no matter how difficult she'd been at times.

"Now. About what I was saying," Rebecca said, but she broke off again and her smile widened when her gaze traveled past Mallory. "Ryan, would you like some punch?"

"This'll do." He reached his arm around Mallory and slipped the glass out of her hand, drinking from it and sending a lurch through her midsection in the process. "Needs some kick, though." His voice was dry.

Mallory felt certain that Rebecca didn't miss the way his fingers slid through hers, but she was simply incapable of letting it bother her. "Who was the man you were talking to?" She didn't see him anywhere now.

"Coleman Black."

Rebecca didn't share Mallory's shock over the name. She looked surprised and a little pleased. "Cole is here? We haven't seen him in months."

"He's outside now talking to Tris and Jefferson. Then he's heading down to see Angel and Brody, though I imagine she'll be the only one actually pleased to see him. You'd better be quick if you want to catch him before he leaves."

Mallory was trying to follow, but was failing miserably. She knew Tristan and Jefferson Clay were Ryan's uncles. Tristan owned CeeVid. And Jefferson had a horse ranch. But what they, or Ryan's cousin, had to do with the man from HW Industries escaped her.

Wondering didn't seem all that important, though, when Ryan tugged her away from his mother toward the doors that led to the corridor outside the gym. "We're going to find ten minutes alone somewhere if it's the last thing I do," he murmured in her ear. "Ever made love in a coat closet?"

"For only ten minutes?" Her tone was dry, but her face felt hot.

His gaze raked down her and it was a wonder it didn't leave a trail of scorch marks on her dress. "The way you look and the way I feel? Darlin', it'll only take five."

Her mouth ran dry. "Then that should leave time for seconds."

He gave a bark of laughter, and hustled her even faster toward the doors. But a bullet in a purple dress crossed their path before they made it.

"Come *on*," Chloe grabbed their hands and tugged. "Santa's passing out the presents from under the tree now!"

Ryan's gaze met hers. *Parenthood,* she mouthed.

He grimaced wryly, and changed course. They followed Chloe to the opposite side of the room, which had become the focus of nearly everyone there. And there was, indeed, a jolly fat man in a Santa suit, doling out the boxes from beneath the tree to every child who, in turn, quickly tore through the wrapping paper and ribbons. Chloe was no exception.

Mallory whispered toward Ryan behind her. "Who provides the gifts?"

There were so many people standing around so closely that probably nobody saw the hand he slid around her waist, his fingers moving dangerously close to her breasts. "Santa," he whispered back.

She stepped her high heel on his toe and he gave a muffled laugh. "CeeVid," he said in her ear, nearly soundless. "Tristan's done it for years now."

She surveyed the excited gift recipients. She'd said Chloe had found a wonderful family, and it seemed to be proven out everywhere she looked. "Who's the Santa?"

"Don't know. Not Tris—he's out talking to Cole."

Mallory's hands settled over Ryan's, keeping his fingers from straying too far and driving her insane. His chest felt solid and warm against her back. And when Chloe triumphantly showed them the trio of learning video games she'd unwrapped, Mallory felt the evening was about as perfect as it could get.

Until she heard a high shriek and Nina VanSlyke's distinctive voice scream, "Dan!"

Chapter Sixteen

"I can't believe Dr. Yarnell proposed like that to Nina in front of everyone." Courtney was still shaking her head the next afternoon over the unexpected culmination of that year's Holiday Festival.

She looked up from the coloring book that she and Chloe were both coloring in. "What if she'd said no? Seriously. He leaves her for weeks on end and comes back before anyone expects him to, dresses up like Santa and sticks a ring in her face? I think she should at least have made him sweat a little." She looked across the table that held nothing but the dregs of a very informal Sunday dinner—pizza and buffalo wings— and eyed Mallory. "What do you think?"

Mallory thought she didn't want to be part of this conversation at all.

But it was Sunday dinner at Emily and Jefferson's place, and of all times, Ryan had finally decided to rejoin the tradition.

How could Mallory have refused?

"I think…maybe Nina's pride wasn't worth passing up what she really wanted," she answered. "Which is obviously Dr. Yarnell." The woman had been clearly overcome when Santa had pulled off his false white beard and the red cap and had presented his last package—a small red box—to her. "It *was* a little romantic," she added. "Grand gesture and all that."

"Nicely summed up," Emily said. On her hip, she was holding a cherubic baby boy who belonged to her son, Axel, and his wife, Tara, who owned the Classic Charms shop that Mallory had found so charming. Though Axel and Tara weren't there because of some other conflict, Emily was obviously delighted to be babysitting.

Mallory fell quiet again. Her gaze kept slipping to Ryan, who was deep in discussion with Evan Taggart over something.

It probably wouldn't be another puppy.

Not since Dr. Yarnell had returned in such dramatic fashion to Nina, summarily ending his sabbatical. Not to mention Mallory's means of staying in Weaver.

She knew Ryan had to understand the consequences of Dan's return. What she didn't know was whether or not he cared.

Because he hadn't said.

And she'd realized how afraid she was of learning the answer if she asked.

That's what happened when those details she let herself overlook jumped up to stare her in the face.

The slice of pepperoni pizza that she'd managed to choke down was sitting uncomfortably in her stomach and she rose from the table, gathering up the used paper plates and empty cups. "Can I get you anything, Gram?"

Kathleen was poring over the photo albums that Gloria had come equipped with and she shook her head. "No thank you, dear."

Mallory glanced around the table, but there were no

other takers, either, and she carried the stack in her hands into the kitchen.

"Trash is here." Rebecca had followed her. With obvious familiarity, she held open a tall cupboard for her.

"Thanks." Mallory stowed the garbage.

"It *was* quite the evening last night."

Mallory nodded jerkily, moved to the sink and washed her hands. She'd have been quite happy to wash dishes if only to keep herself busy, but there were none. Emily had laughed about the disposable nature of their entire meal, blaming it on her grandchildren's unquenchable desire for pizza. Her husband, Jefferson, had just looked amused and suggested it had more to do with the fact that her gift-buying frenzy for those grandchildren had left her with no time for anything else.

When she turned away from the sink, Rebecca handed her a towel. "Would you consider taking a staff position at the hospital?"

Mallory's fingers tightened around the towel at the wholly unexpected question. "I wasn't aware there was one available."

Rebecca's head tilted slightly. "There isn't, exactly. But that isn't to say that there wouldn't be if the board were asked."

Mallory exhaled. She folded the towel and set it next to the old-fashioned farmhouse sink. "Rebecca, you don't have to do that. Just because Dan's back, I'm not going to disappear with Chloe forever. I'll make sure she spends plenty of time here in Weaver."

"I'm not trying to bribe you," Rebecca assured. "I was going to mention it last night, but we were interrupted. Yes, it would be wonderful to have Chloe here permanently. That's purely selfish on my part. But the hospital—the people it serves—can use your skills, Mallory. And I'd like to think that staying in Weaver would suit you, as well. Also selfish on my part, though, because the position wouldn't be able to pay you anything like what you've been earning in New York."

The topic of money was almost funny, considering Mallory hadn't convinced Ryan to take back that check or the trust. Even though she knew what had prompted him, he'd been adamant. And so the envelope containing all of it was still sitting untouched in her office.

Check that. *Dan's* office.

"Just tell me you're interested enough to think about it," Rebecca urged.

"Think about what?" Ryan strolled into the kitchen, with a stack of pizza boxes that he dumped on the counter.

"About Mallory working at the hospital now that Dr. Yarnell has returned."

Her breath stalled in her chest when he looked her way. "Then Chloe wouldn't have to shuttle back and forth."

Right. He was right. But that didn't mean she hadn't held out some wish that he'd notice it meant *she* would be around all the time, too.

She hadn't confused sex with love. But that worked two ways. He wasn't confused, either.

"I have to consider my grandmother, too," Mallory prevaricated. It wasn't entirely untrue. Her grandmother had left behind her circle of friends in New York. And had done it believing that it was temporary.

But the real truth was that, despite her reasoning, her "take what she could get for now" justifications, she knew she would eventually want more from Ryan.

Eventually?

She wanted more right now.

The small pager inside her pocket vibrated, and she yanked it out, absurdly grateful for the distraction as she read the message. "I've got a delivery."

"I'll drive you to the hospital," Ryan said.

Mallory caught the quickly hidden disappointment in Rebecca's eyes. "I wish I'd brought my own car." She glanced at Ryan, only to look away just as quickly. "You could have stayed."

"She could just drive your truck, Ryan," Rebecca suggested. "Then you can stay. And if it gets late, your father and I can drive all of you back."

It made perfect sense. And despite her own longing where Ryan was concerned, she recognized the struggle that worked behind his eyes. Part of him wanted to leave. Part wanted to stay.

But when he pulled his keys out of his pocket and held them toward her, she knew which part had won.

At least there was that.

"Wonderful." Rebecca squeezed Mallory's arm. "And think about it," she urged before leaving the kitchen.

Mallory managed a smile as Ryan dropped his keys in her palm. But he caught her hand. "What's wrong?"

She shook her head. "Nothing."

He looked skeptical. But he didn't argue the point. "Truck's a clutch," he warned instead. "You know how to drive one?"

She nodded and felt an agony of emotion when he used her hand to reel her closer. Just as helpless as a fish, she went, and didn't do anything but kiss him back when his lips found hers.

When he raised his head again, she quickly lifted the keys that she was clutching in her hand. "I'd better get moving or Peggy Duke's baby is going to arrive without me." It was a gross exaggeration; Peggy's first baby would likely take hours yet. "It's probably one of the last calls I'll have," she added, because she couldn't seem to help herself. "Once Dan has a chance to get his calls routed directly to him, again."

She hurried into the living room to say her goodbyes and kiss Chloe, who had no complaints this time whatsoever about Mallory's emergency. Before she could do something really embarrassing, like beg Ryan to feel what he obviously didn't, she grabbed her coat and told him to stay inside where it was warm before hurrying down the wide, shallow steps that led from the imposing door to a wide circular driveway.

He followed, anyway. No coat. No hat. Just tucking his fingers into the front pockets of his blue jeans while the breeze rippled his silver-tipped hair over his forehead and his dark blue shirt against his chest.

"Mallory," he said, when she climbed up behind the wheel.

She managed to get the key in the ignition without dropping it first. "I said I knew how to drive a clutch, and I do, but it's been a while." She knew she was babbling but couldn't help that, either. She made a point of looking down at the pedals and studying the stick. "Don't laugh if I end up popping the clutch."

"I'm not laughing."

No. He was watching her with eyes that were a shade darker than his navy shirt.

And if she didn't leave, she was going to lose it. So she grabbed the door handle and, after a moment that stretched her nerves into a fine wire, he moved out of the way and she closed it.

She was immediately surrounded by his scent. Warmth. Leather. *Him.* It was heady and comforting and sharply painful all at once.

She sucked in air that didn't help that situation at all and turned the key, carefully sketching a casual little wave before putting the truck into gear. She didn't stall it out, nor did she run into any of the other vehicles clustered around the sweeping driveway, but it was a wonder, when her hands were shaking and her vision was blurring.

She drove away from him, from the warmth of the house and those people inside it, and wondered if it felt this terrible now, how would she ever survive leaving for good?

* * *

"You going to stand out here waiting until she comes back again?"

Ryan looked around at his father, who was standing on the porch, smart enough to pull on a coat. "Maybe." The cold feeling in the pit of his stomach wasn't coming from the breeze slicing through his shirt. "At least she *has* to come back," he added more to himself.

"That sounds suspiciously like you're worried she might not." Sawyer's voice floated down to him.

He wasn't up to a verbal chess match with his father. He went up the steps. "I am. Got a cigarette?"

"Nope." Sawyer's lips twisted wryly. "Your mother's getting adamant about 'em. Think having her own grandkid now is making her more opinionated than ever."

Ryan's focus strayed back to the road leading away from the house. There wasn't even any dust that remained from her departure.

"Seems like a nice girl," Sawyer said.

"Chloe?"

"Her, too." His father tilted his head in the direction of the empty, empty road. "But I was talking about your doc."

"She's not *my* anything." Except the mother of his daughter. His lover, except making love once—twice—didn't exactly qualify them for that term. And she was probably the key to his own sanity.

"Do you want her to be?"

His jaw tightened. He didn't answer. And after a moment, his dad sighed. "Talked to Cole for a few minutes last night. Tells me he wants you back pretty badly."

That tack wasn't any more comfortable for Ryan than the subject of Mallory. "Never known him to be all that talkative."

Sawyer's lips twisted. "He and I go back a long way. He goes back a long way with a lot of us. Whether he ever told you or not, he was just as worried as we were when you went missing. Still won't say much about what your last assignment was before you did, though."

"Probably doesn't want to tell you what a bloody mess I made of it." Ryan decided it wasn't all that cold out, after all. Not in comparison to his frozen guts. "And now he figures there's something I can do to fix it?" He shook his head and swore under his breath. "I can't go back, Dad." The admission burned like raw, exposed nerves. "I know I should, but—"

"Who says?" Sawyer clapped his hand over Ryan's shoulder. He was still strong enough, man enough, to make his younger, taller son face him.

"Nobody in this family has ever quit anything," Ryan said roughly. "Except me."

"They've never quit family," Sawyer countered. His brows pulled together. "Not in the end. But there've been times when we've all had to learn to walk away. To let something go. There's no shame in knowing when it's time to do that, son. Sometimes that's the bravest act of all."

Ryan's head felt as if it was in a vise. "There wasn't any honor in what I did. A girl died because of me. A girl nobody even remembers. And more of 'em—" his voice cracked "—more are probably wishing they were dead rather than living through whatever life they've been sold into."

"Honor," Sawyer murmured, "is an interesting thing. Can get tarnished as hell. But it still shines up when you put in the effort. Sort of like families shine up when you work at it. You want to find the honor, Ryan, then make that girl's death count for something. But do it for yourself. Not because you think it's what you've got to do for me. Or for your mother. Or Cole and Hollins-Winword. *We* already know what you're made of." His hand went to the back of Ryan's neck and squeezed and his voice went gruff. "*I* know. And there's never been a day since I've known you that I haven't been proud you're my son." Then his jaw worked and his hand went to Ryan's head, giving him a little shove. "But if you're going to be stupid where *your* doc is concerned, then I might have to sic *my* doc on you."

"How the hell am I being stupid?" He waved his arm. "She says she's in love with me, but she refuses to take anything from me! Not even for Chloe."

"And do you love *her?* Not just because of Chloe? Did you tell her?"

Ryan grimaced, which was obviously answer enough, because his father simply stared at him and slowly shook his head. "God. Somewhere I did go wrong. Women need to hear those words, boy."

"What good will it do? Even when she's offered a chance to work at the hospital now that Yarnell's back, she's not interested! She's going to go back to New York and there's not a damn thing I can do about it."

"Did you ever think about asking her to *stay?*"

"You have a beautiful baby boy." Mallory smiled into Peggy Duke's exhausted face as she held up the little squalling infant.

Peggy was still panting and she pushed up on one elbow to see better. Her other hand was twined around that of her young husband, Drew, who had labored nearly as much as his wife, if Mallory was any judge. "A boy?"

"Perfect in every way," she assured. "Ready to hold him?"

Peggy nodded eagerly. Mallory took the blanket that Lorna, the delivery nurse, handed her. She wrapped it around the baby and settled him in his mother's arms.

"Thank you."

"My pleasure."

But Mallory doubted that Peggy even heard. She was

laughing, tears streaming down her face as she held her son and kissed her husband all at once.

These were the moments that were the best part of Mallory's job.

She'd never felt envious before, but that's what keened through her as she and Lorna finished tending to the new mom. They were all but invisible now, outside the joy bubbling around Peggy and Drew.

Mallory was used to that. And before long, her work was done and she left the delivery room to head for the locker room. The new parents were in their room, probably counting fingers and toes by now, and debating names for their wonderfully perfect son.

She pinched her nose, blinking back the burning behind her eyes.

"Boy or girl?"

She stopped cold, dropping her hand to see Ryan standing in front of the locker-room door. Her heart squeezed up into her throat. "Boy."

"What'd they name him?"

"I don't know," she said faintly. She tugged off her cap and ran her fingers nervously through her hair. Her tennis shoes squeaked against the tile floor as she shifted. "What are you doing here? Did you need your truck?" Peggy's delivery had taken less time than she'd expected, but it had still been several hours.

"I need you."

The cap slid from her fingers and landed soundlessly on the floor.

His eyes focused on hers. "I need you," he repeated. More softly.

Her eyes burned even more. She wasn't capable of this fight. Not right now. Not when everything inside her was aching because she knew that what she really wanted was what couples like Peggy and Drew had.

And she wanted it with Ryan.

"I won't take Chloe away," she said.

"This isn't about Chloe."

"Everything is about Chloe. She's the reason we're here."

"She's not the reason I need you."

She gnawed the inside of her cheek, not daring to let her heart put its own spin on his words. "I'll work here at the hospital. Chloe can…can see you all the time. We'll make it official. Your cousin's husband…the attorney. He can write it up for us."

"We don't need Brody to make this official."

"Why not?" She swallowed hard. "That will of yours is official." The trust account. The check that she would never cash.

"So would be a marriage license."

She winced. He was destroying her. "You don't have to marry me to be her parent, either."

"I do if I want to be *your* husband." His hands closed around her shoulders, burning through the scrubs she wore. "I'm asking you to marry me, Mallory. Take a job here if you want to. Or go back to New York. I don't care, because I'll just follow you!"

She stared. Trying and failing to decipher the glint in his blue, blue eyes. "Chloe—"

"Dammit, Doc, I hate to say this, but if you say our daughter's name one more time right now, I'm going to—"

He let out a noisy breath. Started again. "I love Chloe. I'll probably go to my grave still quaking in my boots, afraid that I'm not as good a father as I know she deserves. But I *need* you." His fingers squeezed her shoulders even harder. "I said I never wanted to feel anything again, but I was already lying to myself. You're the reason I feel again, Mallory. The reason

I *want* to feel again. I want to see your face when I get up in the morning."

She held her breath. Her eyes filled.

His hands gentled. "I want to hold you against me when the day is done." His voice dropped. "And know you're going to be there when we wake up to face a new day all over again."

She inhaled. Shaky. Audibly.

He stepped closer. Bringing with him all of that warmth that had so entranced her from the first moment they'd met. "I want to make love with you and laugh with you and—" his jaw canted to one side and slowly centered again "—and cry with you."

He slid his thumb across her cheek, catching the tears her lashes couldn't contain.

"I want your amazing mind and, most of all, your heart. And I'd want all of that whether Chloe existed or not. But she does, which makes everything even better, and I think she's going to make a helluva big sister."

She let out a laugh that was a good portion sob. "You want more kids?"

"At least you won't have to worry how we'll afford to send them to college." His mouth curved slightly. But his expression was utterly, heart-wrenchingly vulnerable. "You say I know you? Know this. You're the one who's delivered me back into the world of the living, Dr. Keegan. I've never loved anyone the way I love you. I may not know what I'm going to do with my life, but I do know I don't want to do anything without you by my side."

It wasn't a glint in his eyes, she realized.

It was a light.

And she could decipher it after all, even through her tears. Because it was love.

"So." His voice was husky. "Will you marry me?"

She sniffed. Wiped her cheeks. And went onto her toes,

closing her arms around his shoulders. "There's no way we're going back to New York," she whispered thickly. "I'd never have enough time for the *kids* with the schedule they keep me on."

His arms surrounded her. His eyes gleamed. "Is that a yes?"

It was a question. But it was so much more. It was a life, unfolding for them with promise and hope.

She lifted her mouth to his. "Yes."

Epilogue

"R yan." Chloe giggled. "I mean, *Dad.* When are we gonna *go?*"

Ryan's hand tightened around Mallory's. His gaze met hers, wry. Amused. "Don't tell me you're in a hurry to go to bed?"

Chloe rolled her eyes. "It's Christmas Eve." She leaned closer, her hands on Ryan's knees. "Santa's coming," she whispered. As if it were a big secret.

Mallory couldn't seem to get the smile off her face. As far as she was concerned, Santa had already been, and he'd more than delivered. It might have been less than a month since Ryan had first shown up on her doorstep, but she felt as if he'd been part of their hearts forever. "I don't think Santa's going to miss our house if we stay a little longer," she assured Chloe. "It's not even your bedtime, yet."

Chloe exhaled and pushed away again. "This is going to be the longest night *ever,*" she moaned.

But then Zach Forrest crossed her line of vision and, like

a missile, she aimed for him, narrowly missing running into the tall, decorated Christmas tree situated in front of an enormous picture window.

"You know," Mallory mused, studying the tree as she'd done off and on since Ryan had claimed a spot for them to sit after dinner. "That angel topper reminds me of my sister." She smiled faintly. "Isn't that weird?"

He smiled wryly. "Not to me."

They were at the Double-C. The big house, as Ryan had called it. Where Squire and his wife lived with Ryan's uncle, Matthew, and his wife, Jaimie. According to Ryan, it was the only place large enough to hold the really big family gatherings. And Christmas Eve was *really* big.

Watching the faces coming and going from their corner in a deep couch, Mallory still felt a little dazed. "It'll take me forever to get all of their names straight."

Ryan's fingers slid through hers. "We've got forever."

She didn't see how it was possible, but every time he looked at her with emotion so plain in his eyes, her heart just fell open even wider.

"So when's the wedding date?" Axel stopped in front of them, looking all the more masculine for the baby propped against his shoulder. Ryan had told Mallory that Axel would be his best man.

Mallory had asked Courtney to be her maid of honor and Ryan's sister hadn't tried to hide her wet eyes as she'd accepted. "A week from tonight," she answered.

Axel's eyebrows rose and his lips tilted. He patted the padded backside of his tiny son. "New Year's Eve. And I thought Tara and I did fast work. Not bad, Ryan." Someone called his name, and he moved off with a wink.

"It's not too fast, is it?" Ryan looked at Mallory. "There's no time for you to plan some fancy wedding."

"I don't want fancy. I want the people we love there, and

a minister. And we've already been through this." She pushed out of the deeply cushioned couch and held out her hand to him. "Come on. I want some more dessert before it's all gone."

He laughed and rose. "That ain't likely to happen around *this* family." He pressed his mouth to her ear. "You look beautiful."

Heat streaked through her. She supposed that was what she could expect for the next fifty years. Hoped.

"Ahem." The deep voice interrupted them and Mallory felt her face flush as she looked up at Coleman Black. She'd finally learned that he wasn't involved with the family strictly because of Ryan and the others who'd worked for him, but because he was Brody Paine's father.

"You ought to know better than to interrupt a man when he's kissing his fiancée," Ryan commented.

Mallory ignored him and smiled at the man. Yes, he'd been part of the pain of Ryan's past, but he'd also been part of the accomplishment. And if he had never sent that small box of Cassie's things to her, she would never have found her way to Ryan. "Merry Christmas, Mr. Black."

He waved that away. "Cole. Please. And if Ryan ever forgets to appreciate you, let me know and I'll do what I can to set him straight."

She smiled up at Ryan. "I think we're going to be all right."

Cole's gaze was sharp. "Yes. I think you are." He looked at Ryan. "We'll meet next week about your idea," he said. "A network for families to find ones they've lost is something that we all can sink our teeth into."

Mallory squeezed Ryan's hand and shared a look. It wouldn't be the only network of its kind, of course, but it would be all the more powerful for the kind of information that HW Industries could amass.

"We'll talk about it after our honeymoon," Ryan corrected.

Cole smiled. "Right." Then he drew an envelope from

inside his suit and handed it to Ryan. "Here's that other info you asked me to look into." He spotted his daughter-in-law, Angeline, who was lovely in an ivory dress that didn't hide her pregnancy. "Excuse me, won't you?"

He moved off, leaving them alone. Or as alone as they could be in a house teeming with dozens of people, all of whom were related in one way or another to someone else. "It's for you, actually." Ryan handed her the envelope.

She remembered the last one. "What *is* it?"

"Nothing alarming," he assured. "Open it."

Giving him a narrow look, she tore it open and pulled out the folded papers inside and didn't entirely relax until she was certain there wasn't another check inside it, since she'd torn up the other and given it back to him when she'd moved her few belongings out of Dan's office. Until the hospital board voted in January on the new position—which she was assured was a sure thing since a majority of board members came from Ryan's own family—she was officially unemployed.

And found that she didn't mind the break a bit.

"What is all this?" She was flipping through the few pages, all photocopies of old documents and news clippings.

"Hollins conducts detailed background checks on all of its employees," Ryan said. "*Very* detailed."

She peered at the dates on the papers. "Is this yet another relative of yours?"

"Of yours." He put the last sheet—the newspaper article—on top. "That's your father, Mallory." His voice was impossibly gentle. "The information was in Cassie's file."

Her fingers tightened on the sheets. She stared at the grainy text. The even grainier photograph of a handsome young man in uniform. "George M. Cassie." She read the caption. "But how? My mother never told us anything about him. His name wasn't on our birth certificates." She looked at him. "Did Cassie know?"

He shook his head. "I doubt it. There wouldn't have been a reason for her to see her own personnel file. And she'd have told you, wouldn't she?"

She nodded, drawing her finger over the face.

"As for how, it's because Cole hires people who are good at what they do," he said simply. "George died during the fall of Saigon. Before you were born. The article talks about him and the family he helped to escape before he was killed. He was a hero, Doc."

Mallory pressed the papers to her breast and turned into him. "Thank you." Her voice was thick. "I never expected this. It's a wonderful Christmas gift."

"Mom." Chloe was back, pulling at the sleeve of Mallory's red sweater dress. "Come on. Grampa Squire is in the basement and he's passing out presents. To everyone. Grammy's already down there and her present was a bowling ball!" She giggled. "She says she's gonna use it, too, 'cause there's a bowling league on Thursday nights and it's almost *all* old men who don't got girlfriends."

Mallory dashed her hand down her cheek and laughed shakily. Kathleen, it appeared, was planning to fit into Weaver with a vengeance.

"Then we'd better get downstairs, too," Ryan agreed, serious. "Lead the way." He slid his arm around Mallory and pulled her close again. "And after presents, and dessert, *then* can we go home?"

She tucked her head against him and her gaze strayed to the angel at the top of the Christmas tree that stood sentry over the entire celebration.

And she smiled. "Absolutely."

* * * * *

* * *

'THIS EVENING I'm flying to New York for two weeks,'
Jasim imparted with a casualness that made her heart sink
like a stone. 'That's why I had you brought here. I own this
apartment and you'll be comfortable here while I'm abroad.'

'I can afford my own accommodation although I may not
need it for long. I'll have another job by the time you
get back—'

Jasim released a slightly harsh laugh. 'There's no need for
you to look for another position. How would I ever see you?
Don't you understand what I'm offering you?'

Elinor stood very still. 'No, I must be incredibly thick
because I haven't quite worked out yet what you're offering
me.…'

His charismatic smile slashed his lean dark visage.
'Naturally, I want to take care of you.…'

HPEX0110A

'No, thanks.' Elinor forced a smile and mentally willed him not to demean her with some sordid proposition. 'The only man who will ever take *care* of me with my agreement will be my husband. I'm willing to wait for you to come back but I'm not willing to be kept by you. I'm a very independent woman and what I give, I give freely.'

Jasim frowned. 'You make it all sound so serious.'

'What happened between us last night left pure chaos in its wake. Right now, I don't know whether I'm on my head or my heels. I'll stay for a while because I have nowhere else to go in the short term. So maybe it's good that you'll be away for a while.'

Jasim pulled out his wallet to extract a card. 'My private number,' he told her, presenting her with it as though it was a precious gift, which indeed it was. Many women would have done just about anything to gain access to that direct hotline to him, but his staff guarded his privacy with scrupulous care.

Before he could close the wallet, his blood ran cold in his veins. How could he have made such a serious oversight? What if he had got her pregnant? He knew that an unplanned pregnancy would engulf his life like an avalanche, crush his freedom and suffocate him. He barely stilled a shudder at the threat of such an outcome and thought how ironic it was that what his older brother had longed and prayed for to secure the line to the throne should strike Jasim as an absolute disaster....

* * *

What will proud Prince Jasim do if Elinor is expecting his royal baby? Perhaps an arranged marriage is the only solution! But will Elinor agree? Find out in DESERT PRINCE, BRIDE OF INNOCENCE by Lynne Graham [#2884], available from Harlequin Presents® in January 2010.

Bestselling Harlequin Presents author

Lynne Graham

brings you an exciting new miniseries:

PREGNANT BRIDES

Inexperienced and expecting, they're forced to marry

Collect them all:

DESERT PRINCE, BRIDE OF INNOCENCE

January 2010

RUTHLESS MAGNATE, CONVENIENT WIFE

February 2010

GREEK TYCOON, INEXPERIENCED MISTRESS

March 2010

New Year, New Man!

For the perfect New Year's punch,
blend the following:

- *One woman determined to find her inner vixen*
- *A notorious—and notoriously hot!—playboy*
- *A provocative New Year's Eve bash*
- *An impulsive kiss that leads to a night of*
  explosive passion!

When the clock hits midnight Claire Daniels
kisses the guy standing closest to her, but
the kiss doesn't end after the bells stop ringing….

Look for

Moonstruck

by *USA TODAY* bestselling author

JULIE KENNER

Available January

---

red-hot reads

REQUEST YOUR FREE BOOKS!

2 FREE NOVELS PLUS 2 FREE GIFTS!

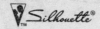

SPECIAL EDITION®

Life, Love and Family!

YES! Please send me 2 FREE Silhouette Special Edition® novels and my 2 FREE gifts (gifts are worth about $10). After receiving them, if I don't wish to receive any more books, I can return the shipping statement marked "cancel." If I don't cancel, I will receive 6 brand-new novels every month and be billed just $4.24 per book in the U.S. or $4.99 per book in Canada. That's a savings of at least 15% off the cover price! It's quite a bargain! Shipping and handling is just 50¢ per book.* I understand that accepting the 2 free books and gifts places me under no obligation to buy anything. I can always return a shipment and cancel at any time. Even if I never buy another book from Silhouette, the two free books and gifts are mine to keep forever.

235 SDN EYN4   335 SDN EYPG

Name	(PLEASE PRINT)	
Address		Apt. #
City	State/Prov.	Zip/Postal Code

Signature (if under 18, a parent or guardian must sign)

Mail to the Silhouette Reader Service:
IN U.S.A.: P.O. Box 1867, Buffalo, NY 14240-1867
IN CANADA: P.O. Box 609, Fort Erie, Ontario L2A 5X3

Not valid to current subscribers of Silhouette Special Edition books.

Want to try two free books from another line?
Call 1-800-873-8635 or visit www.morefreebooks.com.

* Terms and prices subject to change without notice. Prices do not include applicable taxes. Sales tax applicable in N.Y. Canadian residents will be charged applicable provincial taxes and GST. Offer not valid in Quebec. This offer is limited to one order per household. All orders subject to approval. Credit or debit balances in a customer's account(s) may be offset by any other outstanding balance owed by or to the customer. Please allow 4 to 6 weeks for delivery. Offer available while quantities last.

Your Privacy: Silhouette is committed to protecting your privacy. Our Privacy Policy is available online at www.eHarlequin.com or upon request from the Reader Service. From time to time we make our lists of customers available to reputable third parties who may have a product or service of interest to you. If you would prefer we not share your name and address, please check here. ☐

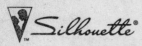

COMING NEXT MONTH
Available December 29, 2009

#2017 PRESCRIPTION FOR ROMANCE—Marie Ferrarella
The Baby Chase

Dr. Paul Armstrong had a funny feeling about Ramona Tate, the beautiful new PR manager for his famous fertility clinic. Was she a spy trying to uncover the institute's secrets…or a well-intentioned ingenue trying to steal his very heart?

#2018 BRANDED WITH HIS BABY—Stella Bagwell
Men of the West

Private nurse Maura Donovan had sworn off men—until she was trapped in close quarters during a freak thunderstorm with her patient's irresistible grandson Quint Cantrell. One thing led to another, and now she was pregnant with the rich rancher's baby!

#2019 LOVE AND THE SINGLE DAD—Susan Crosby
The McCoys of Chance City

On a rare visit to his hometown, photojournalist Donovan McCoy discovered he was the father of a young son. But the newly minted single dad wouldn't be single for long, if family law attorney—and former Chance City beauty queen—Laura Bannister had anything to say about it.

#2020 THE BACHELOR'S NORTHBRIDGE BRIDE—Victoria Pade
Northbridge Nuptials

Prim redhead Kate Perry knew thrill seeker Ry Grayson spelled trouble. It was a case of the unstoppable bachelor colliding with the unmovable bachelorette. But did the undeniable attraction between them suggest there were some Northbridge Nuptials in their near future?

#2021 THE ENGAGEMENT PROJECT—Brenda Harlen
Brides & Babies

Gage Richmond was a love-'em-and-leave-'em type—until his CEO dad demanded he settle down or miss out on a promotion. Now it was time to see if beautiful research scientist Megan Rourke would pose as Gage's fake fiancée…and if their feelings would stay fake for long.

#2022 THE SHERIFF'S SECRET WIFE—Christyne Butler
Bartender Racy Dillon didn't expect to run into her hometown nemesis, Sheriff Gage Steele, in Vegas—let alone marry him in a moment of abandon! Now they were headed back to their small town with a big secret…but was there more to this whiplash wedding than met the eye?

SSECNMBPA1209